Waiting for Ana

Annie Seaton

Sunshine Coast Series: 1

ANNIE SEATON

This book is a work of fiction. Names, characters, places, and incidents are the product of the author's imagination or are used fictitiously. Any resemblance to actual events, locales, or persons, living or dead, is coincidental.

Second Edition: Waiting for Ana, 2021

ISBN 978-0-6450584-6-8

Dedication

To my readers who love my books set in our fabulous Australian towns and country landscapes.

Acknowledgement

Thank you to Anna Welch for her accurate proofreading!

Chapter One

"Ouch." Anastasia Delaney dropped the hammer and put her thumb up to her mouth. It was sure to bruise from the thump she'd just given it. There was only one more length of decorative beading to nail up around the window frame and then she would have to leave for the meeting she was dreading so much.

The years had flown by since she and her two best friends had started the restoration department at Joe Hickey's little hardware store in Maleny, up the mountain from the Sunshine Coast. Ana had spent years in her Gramps' tool shed when she was growing up there and had a natural talent for working with wood. Sienna was the artist who worked on the delicate mouldings and painting. Her twin sister, Georgie, was the jack-of-all-trades who could turn her hand to any task. Their reputation had grown, and they always had plenty of jobs booked in the old cottages along the coast. Ana loved nothing more than working with friends she'd known since school. She blinked back a tear at the pain in her thumb and the thought that this could be their last restoration job together.

"I'll miss this so much once the takeover goes through and our department is shut down. We do damn good work, girls." Ana ran her hand lovingly over the highly polished window frame. "It's just unfair. Why does everything have to be about making money these days? We use quality materials and look at the fabulous work we do. It absolutely pees me off."

"Don't be so negative." Sienna wandered in from the balcony and stood beside Ana. "We're not going to give up until we know for sure our jobs are gone."

Georgie frowned from the top of the ladder where she was hanging curtains at the other end of the bay window. "Ana. We've got no chance if you're late for the appointment with the CEO of Home and Hardware. You should have left already. And you haven't even changed. You can't go looking like that."

"Changed?" Ana brushed the sawdust from her sleeves. "What's wrong with my work clothes? I'm a tradesperson, and I'm happy to look like one. If he judges us on the way we dress—"

"No, listen to me, girlfriend. You are a successful businesswoman and you're meeting with the top bloke from the biggest chain of home improvement stores in the country. He might also be our future boss." Sienna reached into her pocket and there was a crafty smile on her face as she held up a set of car keys. "I know what you're like, so I came prepared. Not only are you taking my car, but you will find a suit and heels waiting for you on the back seat." With a languorous wave of the paint brush she was holding in her other hand, Sienna stared at Ana. "My sporty little car will impress the hot shot executive."

Ana looked down at her paint-splattered overalls and sighed. "Maybe you should be the one to go and convince him not to shut us down. You've got the class I am sadly lacking."

And the courage, she thought to herself.

Sienna waited for Georgie to climb down the small ladder and then she put the paintbrush on the bottom rung. "Ana, we've been over this before. You knew this guy at uni, so that has to give us a bit more bargaining power."

"Blake Buchanan worshipped the dollar when we were at UQ, so I don't think we'll have any chance of him changing his mind about closing our department." Ana sat on one of the upturned buckets and looked up gratefully as Georgie passed her a bottle of water. "And I didn't mention it before, but we parted on bad terms so that will probably give us even less chance of our jobs surviving." She turned to the large window which looked out over the water. The ocean was a sheet of silver with not a breath of breeze ruffling it. Half a dozen surfers waited for waves on the point, and as she watched a pod of dolphins frolicked around them.

'Oh wow, look that means good luck!' The magnificent view calmed her nerves a little as she sipped the cool water. She didn't want the twins to know she and Blake had been more than mere acquaintances when they'd lived in the share house at Toowong he'd owned ten years ago. Even though they'd both been studying for a business degree, their philosophies had been very different. Blake's emphasis on conservative economics had been at odds with her study of welfare economics and they'd eventually agreed to disagree when their arguments became too heated. Their discussions had been stimulating and Ana had loved sparring with him. Most evenings she would bait him with a provocative comment about her day in class just to get a rise out of him. He was so passionate about his beliefs he fell for it every time. She'd loved watching his eyes darken and his sexy mouth lift in a smile when he realised she was teasing him. She had instigated many a discussion just so she could watch his face come alive. And she'd fallen a little more in love with him the longer she stayed in the house.

"We were absolute opposites in everything, and we fought like cats and dogs," Ana explained to her friends. "He even listened to classical music. I mean, who does that when you're young? That was my heavy metal stage and it drove him crazy."

"What else?" Sienna's beautifully made up eyes were fixed on Ana's face.

"You know how I love football?" she continued. "I used to go to the games at Suncorp with the other guys and Blake would be off playing golf or something equally as snooty."

Georgie giggled. "Are you sure you aren't being too hard on him? You did go through a pretty wild stage at uni."

"It all came to a head, one night after we'd been to a State of Origin game. We came home and Blake was waiting on the porch and he read me the riot act about the state of my room. God, even Mum didn't do that."

Sienna picked up her paintbrush, her eyes narrowed. "Maybe your mother should have?"

"Thanks, sweets." Ana shook off the criticism like water off a duck's back. She was used to being teased by the girls. She'd lived in a mess at uni when she was busy studying—and having a good time— and she still lived in chaos these days. There just wasn't enough time to run a business and finish restoring her old cottage. Keeping everything tidy didn't pay the bills.

'So what happened?' Georgie asked.

Ana pulled a face. "I'd had a couple of beers at the game, so I told Blake he had no right to be in there, called him a sexist pig and slammed the front door in his face. I locked him out of his own house." She smiled at the memory. "The other guys went to bed and Blake sat outside, cooling his heels until I let him back in. Then I got the call from the hospital about Mum the very next day and moved home. You know the rest."

Actually, they didn't.

They knew she'd given up in her final year of university to come home and nurse her mother through the final stages of breast cancer, but she'd never told anyone about that night with Blake. It was a delicious memory; one she'd pulled out and relived during the tough nights when her mother had been dying.

When she'd decided to let him back in, Blake had been sitting on the front steps looking across the road at the muddy Brisbane river and he'd ignored the open door behind him. Ana had stood quietly for a moment drinking in the sight of him before she'd called to him softly.

"Blake. I've opened the door for you." His broad shoulders strained beneath his white polo shirt and his dark hair curled over the collar. A shaft of pure longing shot through her.

Ana's fingers had itched to run through his hair, and she'd fought the urge to go and sit on the step next to him in the moonlight. It had been one of those still Brisbane nights, and was late enough that the main road was clear of the usual noisy traffic.

"What are you looking at?" he'd asked.

What? Did he have eyes in the back of his head?

Heat had suffused her face at the thought of being caught checking him out and she covered up her discomfort with a teasing laugh.

"I was just wondering if it was safe to let you back in. Or have I pushed your buttons again?"

Slowly, Blake had pushed himself to his feet and turned around. Ana had edged back through the door, unable to read the look on his face in the shadows, but his stance was predatory. In one swift movement, he'd jumped up the last step and before she could get inside, he'd pinned her against the wall of the porch and Ana had tried to cover up the feelings rioting through her with a nervous giggle.

"Let go." She half-heartedly tried to pull away, but he'd laced his fingers through hers and held her hands above her head.

"Anastasia, you always push my buttons, without even trying."

She'd been trapped between Blake and the wall, and when she'd looked up at him, her breasts had pressed into his hard chest. With a soft groan, he'd lowered his head and gently slid his lips across her cheek. "You drive me crazy; do you know that?"

With each word his mouth had come closer to hers and now hovered over her lips. "The way you walk, your voice, your laugh, that hippy perfume you wear. I can't get you out of my head."

She'd smiled at him and eased her arms from his loose grasp, taking his face between her hands. 'I can't stop thinking about you either, Blake," she'd whispered. "And I'm sorry I called you a sexist pig."

That first kiss they'd shared on the front porch had been slow and soft. The feel of Blake's warm mouth on hers was everything Ana had dreamed of and she'd closed her eyes as a delicious languor drifted through her. She'd sensed he was holding back and that it was up to her to let him know it was okay to take it further.

Finally, she'd smiled against his mouth and murmured. "My room or yours?"

He'd lifted his head and even in the dim light she could see the laughter lines crinkle around his eyes and the warmth stirred low in her belly as he'd held her gaze.

"Is your bed clear?"

"It's made, but it's covered in . . .er . . .stuff."

"I guess it's my room then."

##

"So are you going to stand there daydreaming all afternoon, or are you going to go to Noosa and save our jobs?" Ana jumped when Sienna dangled the keys in front of her face.

"All right, I'm going. But be prepared for disappointment. Blake was a nice guy, but when it came to business profit, margins always came first."

Georgie rolled her eyes. "Ana, I have been trying to tell you that for years. You can't expect a small business to support every philanthropic activity."

"Well, Joe does." The owner of the local hardware store which employed them turned a blind eye to a lot of the work they never billed out to the older residents in the community. Joe's family had opened the first general store in Main Street, Maleny in the 1920s and he loved his hometown with a passion. "I can't understand why he had to sell the business anyway, *and* to a huge corporation."

Sienna stared at Ana. "Well, he's almost eighty-years-old. He has no children to take over the store, and he and Magda deserve a nice retirement. She was looking at cruise brochures just the other day." She nudged Georgie and winked. "She said she might as well read something because she was sick of waiting for our accounts to come in."

"All right, all right. No need to be a smart arse. I'll do them tonight." Ana reached for Sienna's keys "I *will* finish them, and when Blake comes to the store, we can show him how much business we pull in. That will convince him to keep us on. Besides the community needs us."

Sienna yawned. "Two problems with that, Ana. You're the one meeting with him, and I have a feeling that may be the only meeting that happens. And do you really think a big company like Home and Hardware will care about the local community? Maybe it's time we faced reality and accept we're all going to be out of a job." She folded her arms and gazed out the window. "I have enough put away that I can manage for a few months. I've already been offered a couple of days work in the art gallery at the top of the main street."

Disappointment pressed on Ana's chest like a dead weight. It sounded like her friends had accepted that their work was about to end. "Well, whatever you decide, Georgie and I can still keep the business running." She turned toward the front door full of renewed determination. "I hate change. I really do."

Georgie cleared her throat.

Ana turned around and groaned. "Oh, no. Not you too, Georgie?"

"It's just a backup. Just in case you can't convince your Blake."

"He's not my Blake," Ana snapped. "And what plans have you made?"

"Joe told me there will be a position in the new store for me. He knows I don't mind being in the store when we don't have renovation jobs."

Ana came back across the room and draped her arms around the shoulders of the two women who were her best friends in the whole world. Since her mother had died, she had no other family and she'd filled the emptiness with her work. Sienna and Georgie and her elderly friends in Maleny were her life.

"It's okay. I'm being selfish. Like I said, I hate change. But I will convince Blake to keep us on, anyway. No matter what it takes."

Sienna grinned at her with a wicked glint in her eye. "No matter what it takes?

Ana folded her arms and nodded. There was no way she was going to let her friends and the community down.

##

Two hours later, Ana parked Sienna's two-seater red sports coupe right outside a modern two storey house on a canal at Noosa, thanking whoever was looking out for her. A parking space here was like gold any time of day or night.

Raindrops glistened in the soft afternoon sunlight and reflected a rainbow of colours across the glass front of the house. A typical Sunshine Coast storm had hit and cleared as she'd driven down the mountain, Ana sat in the car for a moment and closed her eyes trying to calm her nerves as the memory of Blake kissing her the last time she'd seen him came storming back

She was sure she'd been a one night fling to him, but she'd followed his stellar rise in the business world with interest after he'd gone to Melbourne and finished his MBA. Okay, maybe her Internet searches were more than a passing interest, more like a hunger to fill the emptiness where her heart had once been. Last time she'd Googled him, he'd been managing a wilderness retreat in North Queensland. After that she had made herself stop cyberstalking him—it wasn't healthy, and she had plenty to fill her life without dreaming of an old unrequited love.

"Get out of the car. You're not twenty anymore." She opened her eyes and took a deep breath. All her old insecurities had come rushing back. "It doesn't matter that you don't have a degree. You're a successful businesswoman, now act like one."

So what if my dreams of a corporate career and an MBA were history?

She'd had a precious six months with Mum before she died, and her life had turned out just fine without a bachelor's *or* master's degree. So maybe she didn't have a stellar Fortune 500 career like Blake and some of the others from their share house in Brisbane, but the little enterprise she, Georgie, and Sienna had set up was successful and fulfilling.

Who knows what might have come after our night together if I'd stayed and we'd talked?

The next morning, after Blake had gently kissed her goodbye and left for his early class, the ringing of the house phone had woken her.

"Can you come home, Ana? It's not looking good." Her mother's words were still imprinted on her mind.

My mother, my beautiful mother. Nothing else had mattered in that moment.

She'd run into her room, showered and packed; within an hour, she'd called a taxi to get her to the bus station. Overcome by worry and grief for her mother, she hadn't even left a note.

After Mum had passed, she'd briefly considered going back to uni, but by that time, she and the twins had started up their restoration business. She knew Blake had moved to Melbourne to take a position in one of the top firms in the investment business and she was determined to forget about him.

And now here she was, in her best friend's sports car dressed in a borrowed business suit, a pair of borrowed Jimmy Choos, her stomach churning, and about to confront Blake, to convince him not to close their little business as part of the takeover of the Maleny hardware store by the national corporation he represented.

"Shit." Water gushed into her shoe as she stepped out of the car straight into a puddle from an overflowing drain. Sienna would kill her. "Focus," she muttered to herself, bending to remove the ruined footwear. "One wet shoe is the least of my worries." It wasn't just the thought of her friends losing their jobs that was making her feel ill.

Pull yourself together. It was just a crush. Just one night.

She'd had several short relationships over the years but none of them had stayed in her heart like that one night with Blake. She pulled her thoughts together. They were so different, it never would have worked out anyway, even if Mum hadn't got sick.

She tucked Sienna's shoes under her arm, swallowed, and pushed open the gate.

Chapter Two

Blake Buchanan sat at his small work desk in the study, annoyed that his four o'clock appointment was late. It had been a long week full of meetings with suppliers, and Zoom meetings with Mike, the owner of Home and Hardware. All he had to do now was get this last appointment out of the way and then he intended pouring a red wine from his well-stocked cellar. He was keen to shed the business suit and get into a comfortable pair of jeans. The email from his secretary had been brief and he only knew that the guy he was about to meet was a restoration specialist at the Maleny store. That whole department would go in the takeover. Blake had been Chief Executive Officer at Home and Hardware for the past three years, and shedding personnel was just another part of the job to him. Nothing to lose any sleep over.

Returning to Noosa meant being close to family—even though there was only his sister, Jeannie, her husband Rod, the local vet, and their tribe of kids left, he was determined to settle back into the town he'd grown up in. He'd had the house on the canal built last year and now he looked around it with pleasure. Glass walls across the back of the house gave him an uninterrupted view of the canal.

He couldn't help but think of Anastasia Delaney when he looked at the water. She'd grown up on the Sunshine Coast too, even though they hadn't met until they were in Brisbane at uni and she applied for a place in his share house. She'd been the only girl in the house and the most disorganised person he had ever met. She'd driven him crazy with the chaos that she'd created and her idealistic economic views.

But what a beauty she'd been, blonde and lithe. And her carefree spirit and her joyful approach to life had brought the share house alive. Blake's parents had been quiet, and if he was honest, a little bit stuffy, and he knew he had been turning into a lonely and boring adult. The move back here was the time for him to change and start enjoying life.

Back in those days, he'd watched Ana from a distance as she'd gone out with the other guys and envied the fun they had together. Until that night she'd locked him out and they ended up in his bed.

The next afternoon on the way back from lectures, he'd bought a huge bunch of brightly-coloured flowers, and anticipation had filled him as he'd waited for her to come home from her part-time job at the coffee shop in Paddington. Finally, after waiting for hours, he'd checked her room, and he still remembered the hollow ache in his gut when he'd seen the stripped bed and empty closet.

When she didn't get in touch with him, the anger kicked in. She'd been toying with him and was obviously as loose with her relationships as she was in the rest of her life. Everyone in their house lost touch with her from that day.

But she stayed firmly fixed in his mind until he left for his job in Melbourne. He couldn't understand why she'd dropped out of uni so suddenly and he'd often wondered if she'd finished her degree somewhere else. And he couldn't let go of that niggling guilt that sleeping with him had caused her to flee. It hadn't made sense because she'd murmured sleepily for him to hurry back when he'd had to leave for his early lecture. And he thought she had enjoyed the night of gentle passion as much as he had.

He hadn't thought about her for a long time.

She's probably married and still lurching from one disaster to another. Maybe he could look her up now that he was back on the coast. He was determined to have a life which allowed time for some fun. His job had been boring him lately and he intended to do something about that as soon as this takeover was completed.

Blake glanced down at his watch in annoyance, and then he stood and moved across to the window as the sound of a car engine reached him.

About time.

A red BMW Z3 was parked outside his house. A firm derriere and long legs with shapely calves were visible as a woman in a red suit bent down beside the car and removed her shoes. His heartbeat kicked up a notch as a cascade of silvery blonde hair swung forward hiding her face from his view. For a fleeting moment, the sight took him back ten years. The unusual silver-coloured hair reminded him of Anastasia—strange when he'd just been thinking about her. There was no way it would be her. She'd hated all the trappings of wealth. Fancy cars, exclusive addresses, and what she'd called 'fancy do dads' provided the catalyst for some of their more interesting . . . and fiery . . . debates. She'd always go on about giving back to those who didn't have as much and helping those who were unable to help themselves. He shook his head wondering what she'd done with her life and if reality had helped her outgrow her naive beliefs. He'd never been able to agree with her soft approach.

If you wanted something, you worked for it. It was as simple as that. If you didn't, you didn't get it.

He dropped the curtain, irritated with the direction of his thoughts and picked up his phone to read the headlines. Anastasia was in the past and now he would give this guy five more minutes to turn up before he missed his chance to make whatever argument he was going to try to convince Blake to keep the restoration department. The meeting was a waste of time anyway—there was no place for non-existent profit margins in the new financial model.

Just as he became engrossed in the news, the doorbell rang. Blake stood and put his phone in the charger on his desk on the way past.

About time.

Straightening his tie, he moved across to the door, and glanced through the window. The BMW was still there but the Anastasia lookalike had disappeared. Schooling his face to reflect a conservative businessman, he opened the door to his late appointment. It was like a punch in the stomach and he struggled to catch his breath as the fragrance of patchouli oil drifted across from the silver-headed woman standing on the front porch.

"Hello, Blake." The sweet voice reminded him he was staring, and he gathered himself together as she reached out to grip his arm. "Blake?"

"Anastasia." He stared at her, taking in the red business suit and the designer bag tucked beneath her arm. It was a more sophisticated look than the flowing skirts and jangling bracelets of the girl who'd lived in his house, but she was still drop dead gorgeous and his heart rate took off. The hippy perfume of the share house days wafted around him, at odds with the classy outfit.

"What . . . when . . . how did you know I had moved back to Noosa? My God . . . Anastasia. What are you doing here? It must be ten years—"

"Yes, it's been ten years since I left. A long time, Blake." She removed her hand from his arm, hitched her bag onto her shoulder and looked steadily at him.

He stared at her, lost for words for a moment and then his brain kicked back into gear.

"How did you know I was back here?"

"You've come to take over the hardware store down at Maleny." Her expression was hard to read.

"You must have read the article in the *Financial Review*," he said slowly.

The paper had done an interview about his corporate success and anyone who read it would know how wealthy he was now. Experience had taught him to be wary of people who sought him out, seemingly out of the blue. Straightening his shoulders, he stepped back. "Come in. I have an appointment scheduled, but he's late so he's missed out." He'd give her a few minutes to explain why she was here and then she could tell him where the hell she'd disappeared to that morning. "You know I tried to find you after you left, but no one knew where you had gone. I even tried calling all the Delaneys on the coast. Why did you just take off like that?" As much as he tried to keep his voice short and business like, he couldn't help the surge of feeling that warmed him as she stood beside him. That damn perfume was taking over his senses and his head was ten years in the past, not to mention his body.

"You tried to find me?" Her voice was soft, and he lost his train of thought for a moment as her clear blue eyes gazed steadily at him.

"I owed you an apology. The way I spoke to you that night was way out of line. And then . . . the next day . . . after we . . . after that night . . . you were gone when I came home."

God, he was as tongue-tied as a teenager on his first date.

"All water under the bridge now." She smiled at him, tucking her hair behind her ear and his mood softened as her hand shook a little. "Blake, I need to talk to you. Look, I am your app—"

Before she could finish, a loud screech of tyres signalled the arrival of a familiar white SUV, which turned into the narrow driveway at the front of the house. A taxi followed and parked behind it. Blake groaned.

What the hell is Jeannie up to now?

His sister was the grand master of madcap schemes and although he loved the time he spent with her and her family, this was not the time for one of her madcap ideas. He wanted to know why Ana had come to see him, and he didn't need Jeannie's interruption.

All those thoughts flew from his head when his sister jumped out of her SUV. Her face was streaked with tears. She looked up at him wordlessly over the low gate that edged the short path in front of the house.

"Excuse me." He turned to Ana before he hurried down the stairs. "Don't go anywhere."

He vaulted over the low metal gate to the driveway. By the time he reached his sister, she was handing a small suitcase to the cab driver.

"What's the matter? What are you doing?" He opened his arms to her, and Jeannie leaned into him. Her whole body was shaking.

His stomach clenched and fear crawled into his throat. He placed his hands on her arms, gently pushing her back so he could see her face. Her eyes red-rimmed and awash with tears, Jeannie passed a shaking hand through her short black curls.

"It's Rod. The light plane he's on is missing. They're out searching now." She hiccupped and caught her breath. "I just got the call."

"Where was he?"

"He was flying back to the lodge from a fishing trip with a group of guys. I'm booked on a flight to Cairns and it leaves in an hour. The kids are in the car and I threw in some food and clothes for them." She reached up and kissed him on the cheek, before handing him a set of car keys.

"I'm so glad you're here now, I don't know what I would have done if you had still been in Melbourne. I'll call you as soon as I get there."

Before he could answer, Jeannie climbed into the taxi and told the driver to hurry to the airport.

"Anything you need, just get it delivered." His sister waved to him from the open window as the taxi backed quickly out of the driveway and accelerated down the street. Blake turned to the SUV when the loud bellow of a baby came through the partially open window. Reaching for the door, he looked up when the gate squeaked.

"I couldn't help overhearing." Anastasia hurried over to him. "Tell me how I can help?"

Blake was used to dealing with corporate takeovers and crises in the business place but was completely at a loss standing in his own driveway with a carload of kids. He ran his hand through his hair and turned to Anastasia.

"I guess we'd better take them inside."

***

The blood had hummed in Ana's ears when Blake opened the door and she'd fought the urge to turn tail and run back to Sienna's car. He'd barely changed in ten years. His jet black hair was shorter but as dark as ever, although she'd glimpsed a sprinkle of grey when they were outside. A few little wrinkles around his eyes added maturity to his face, but apart from that he was still the Blake of her memories. She'd focused on looking calm, ignoring the heat that rushed through her fingertips when she touched his arm. The business clothes helped her confidence, although being in stockinged feet with wet shoes tucked beneath her arm did detract from the sophistication.

Her heart went out to Jeannie. Fear had been etched into her face, and her voice had broken when Blake had held her. Ana had met Jeannie briefly when she'd been at college and all her nervousness disappeared as she thought about how to help her. And if the look on Blake's face was any indication, he had no idea what to do with a crying baby.

"Unlock the door." She spoke confidently to convey the impression that she did know what to do, but, she was clueless about kids, too.

Blake double clicked the remote in his hand and all the windows of the car slid down. A combination of cries, chattering, and barks became instantly louder. A baby of an indeterminate age, strapped in a rear-facing car seat, was screaming. She had a pink T-shirt on, so Ana assumed it was a girl. Two small boys who looked to be the same age were arguing over an action hero, the noise punctuated by the sharp barks of a large bloodhound whose tongue was hanging over the tops of their heads as he turned from one to the other, lathering drool across the leather seat.

"It's mine . . . give it to me." The struggle escalated as a tug-of-war battle ensued over the action figure.

"No! It's mine." The boy on the far side burst into tears as an arm pulled out of the figure's torso. "Now, look. You broke Spider-Man. I hate you."

The young girl sitting in the front seat looked up calmly from her book and spoke through the open window.

"Don't worry, Uncle Blake. He always says that, and Mummy tells him not to. So he will be in big trouble when she comes back with Daddy."

Ana blinked away the tears pricking her eyes at the certainty in the little girl's voice. Blake appeared to be incapable of moving or speaking, so she decided it was time to take over. One of the staff at the store had gone into shock one day from an allergic reaction, and Blake had the same look about him.

"Blake, you get the boys out of the back and I'll take the baby." She turned to the young girl in the front. "What's your name, sweetie?"

"Madeleine and I am eight-years-old. I'm the oldest. My twin brothers are six."

"Okay, Madeleine, can you climb out and help Uncle Blake get the boys out?"

Madeleine smiled sweetly at Ana and opened the door. The dog chose that moment to take a flying leap over two rows of seats and make a break for it.

"Get the dog." Ana yelled at Blake, grabbing helplessly at the dog's collar as it pushed past her. Blake jerked out of his stupor and tackled the dog before it could take off down the road.

Ana opened the back door and undid the baby's seat belt before lifting her out. She wrinkled her nose at the smell.' Oh dear.'

One of the boys giggled. "That's why he's crying. He hates sitting in poo."

"He?" asked Ana. "I thought he was a girl."

The two boys, who Ana now realised were identical twins, giggled in unison. "Maddy dressed him. She wants a little sister and all she got were us brothers." Obviously, they both thought this was a subject of great hilarity. Maddy glared at them as she stood quietly next to the car, clutching a book in her hand.

"Come on, guys. Let's go inside." Blake attempted to brush the dirt and wet grass off his trousers with one hand while he clutched the dog's collar with the other.

"Ah, he speaks," said Ana trying to lighten the mood. She looked up at Blake and tried to give him a reassuring smile. Settling the baby on her hip, she took the hand of one of the boys. "I'll help you get everyone to the house, Uncle Blake, and then you can introduce me to these lovely children."

Blake mouthed a silent thank you to her, before turning to the gate, the dog's collar in one hand and the small hand of one twin in the other. Ana followed him, stepping carefully in her stockinged feet. The last thing she wanted was to slip on the wet path and do a face plant into the hedge, baby and all. She and the kids traipsed up the narrow stairs and they crowded onto the small glass-sided landing.

"I think it would be better if you take them in and get them settled. They don't know me, so I'll unpack the car." She passed him a disposable nappy. "This was on the seat. You change the baby while I get the food. That'll be the first thing they need, I guess?"

"Thanks. I've never changed a nappy in my life."

Ana grinned at him as she held her hand out for the car keys. "Time to learn." She ran lightly down the stairs to the driveway. The afternoon sun had dried the steps and path, and she took a deep breath appreciating the salt-tanged breeze drifting up from the ocean. She opened the back of the SUV and surveyed the crates piled in front of her.

Where to start?

She reached forward to a crate jammed with groceries and jumped when the blanket to her right shifted and the music from *Baby Shark* blared out.

"Hello." A pair of large brown eyes peered out from beneath the blanket.

Ana placed her hand on her chest. That explained the empty booster seat in the third row of the SUV. He must have unbuckled himself during all the commotion.

"Oh my goodness, another one. Who are you?"

"I'm Billy. B-I-L-L-Y. I can spell my name and I'm only four and this is Fred and Wilma."

My God, how many children are in this family?

He lifted the blanket and Ana exhaled a sigh of relief at the sight of two tiny kittens curled up together in a box.

"Okay, Billy, let's get you inside."

"No. I'm going to wait here for Mummy. She's going to get my Daddy."

Ana's eyes pricked again, and she thought for a moment, for anything she could use to entice Billy out of the car. "I think the kitties would like a drink. Can you come and help me?"

"No."

"How about we go in for something to eat in Uncle Blake's house."

"No."

She reached out and tried to take the little boy's hand, but he whimpered and backed into the corner and pulled the blanket over his head, drumming his heels on the floor of the car. Ana climbed into the back of the wagon, hitched Sienna's skirt down, while racking her brain for any ideas to persuade him to get out of the car. She settled in next to Billy before gently lifting the blanket and peeking beneath it. He ignored her, playing his game intently with his little fingers flying over the touch screen.

"Oh no," exclaimed Ana. "Your iPad's running out of battery, do you think we'd better go inside and plug it in?"

"Oh yes . . . only nineteen left," he said. Billy clasped the iPad to his chest and slid out of the car past her, pushing the gate open just as Blake ran through the door with a worried look on his face.

"Oh, thank goodness, I just remembered Billy."

Ana swallowed a smile as she climbed out of the car and held up the cat box. "I found him—and Fred and Wilma."

Blake took Billy and a few of the larger bags inside and Ana went back to the car. It took her a few minutes to carry an assortment of soft bags, plastic crates, a portable cot and toys and put them on the front porch. It amazed her that Jeannie had been able to remember to pack all that after getting the phone call about her husband. All was quiet inside and she assumed that Blake was feeding the children in the kitchen. Ana slid the bags and crates into the living room off the formal entry and looked around at the room with admiration.

It was very different to the house they'd shared in Brisbane. No worn carpet and mismatched furniture. No smell of sweaty shoes and gym gear and basketballs. The perpetual chaos of their college house had driven Blake crazy and he'd spent much of his time picking up after everybody. The house was very different to the old house in Brisbane and the cottage-type interiors Ana preferred, but the minimalist decorating suited Blake. The pristine white leather lounges and the gleaming hardwood floors complemented each other. The soft afternoon light streaming in through the sheer blinds reflected off the glass sculpture on the large coffee table.

Blake came in from the back of the house, a harried look on his face. "Ana, I owe you big time. Thanks so much for unpacking the car." His gaze ran over the piles of bags and crates and she could have sworn he blanched.

What the hell was Blake going to do with five children, a dog, two cats—not to mention the goldfish she'd found in a large screw top jar in one of the crates—in a spectacular home like this? It was not a home for children to run wild in, and by the look of these kids, they were keen to get moving. She grinned at him and fought the chuckle that was rising in her throat. "I suggest you find one room and keep them contained, otherwise these five little whirlwinds and their assorted pets are going to put their stamp on your house very quickly."

"I'll cope with them the best I can. Jeannie needs me."

Ana hesitated. It wasn't the right time to talk about the store, and Blake still didn't seem to realise she was his four o'clock appointment. For the sake of old times, and their old friendship, the least she could do was help him out. And who knew, helping him might go towards softening him up when she found the right time to discuss business later.

"I'm sure you'll be fine," she said. "I remember you used to be able to cope with most things back in our uni days. I'll just go out and lock Jeannie's car."

Smothering a grin at the look on Blake's face, Ana turned to the door. Mr. Hot Shot CEO had disappeared. She had a feeling he was about to transform into Mr. Mum.

"You're not leaving?" He reached out and touched her arm and she ignored the flutters in her belly.

"No, I'm not leaving."

***

Relief coursed through Blake as Anastasia headed out to lock the car. She was staying and he would have someone to help, as well as have time to talk to her. If he'd heard her correctly in all the confusion, she'd said *she* was his appointment. Could his secretary have messed up his calendar somehow? There was no way Anastasia was going anywhere until they had a talk and he found out why she'd turned up on his doorstep, all dressed up and sophisticated.

Before he could get his head around the situation, two small arms grabbed his legs.

"*Unca* Blake, it's bath time." He looked down at the earnest little face of his nephew and groaned. Billy's mouth and cheeks were smeared with peanut butter. Taking a small hand in his, he led his nephew into the family room and kept a hold on him while he scooped baby Jake up from the floor. He didn't want peanut butter—or baby poo— all over the house.

"Come on you guys, Billy says it's bath time." He headed upstairs, shaking his head as the small entourage of children followed him.

He felt like the Pied Piper.

I can deal with this. As long as Rod is okay.

36

But a frisson of excited anticipation curled in his stomach as he waited for Ana to come back inside.

Chapter Three

Ana spent a few minutes outside to gather her thoughts after she locked the car. She would help Blake out, just as she would for any of her friends, and her own needs would be set aside in the meantime. She looked in the kitchen after she came inside but there was no sign of anyone. The sound of children giggling drew her upstairs. A trail of clothes led to a large bathroom and she peeked around the open door. Blake had discarded his tie and stood next to the bath with his sleeves rolled up; water dripped from his hair onto his white business shirt. The black and white tiled floor was awash with soap suds and Blake ducked as a stream shot out at him from a water pistol which appeared from beneath a huge mound of bubbles in the centre of the bath.

He noticed her peering around the door and grinned. Her mouth dried at the sight of his unbuttoned shirt, dark hair peeking through the V, and his chest clearly outlined by the wet silk.

She cleared her throat. "What's going on here?"

A chorus of voices from the bathtub greeted her as four little heads popped up through the deep bubbles. Ana looked around the room curiously as she walked across the floor.

"Where's the baby?"

"Asleep. The poor little guy was exhausted, and he fell asleep on me when I lifted him out of the bath. He's wrapped in a dry towel and on the floor in my room. I didn't want to wake him."

Blake smiled at her, looking quite pleased with himself.

"I'll get the others out of the bath while you go down and get the portable cot. I don't know much about babies but I'm pretty sure they need to be dressed and not left asleep on the floor."

Blake shrugged as Ana reached over to slide a towel from the warming rack beside the bath. She slipped on the soapy floor and bumped into Blake's hard chest. He grabbed her arms to steady her and her cheek brushed the wet silk.

"Thank you." She straightened and pulled away before she stared at the wet shirt in front of her nose. "But why are you bathing the rest of the children?"

She fought another chuckle as he looked at her with confusion.

"They asked for a bath," Blake said.

"We love Uncle Blake's big deep tub," said Maddy. "Mummy let us swim last time we stayed here before Uncle Blake came home."

"Guess I got conned," he said softly as his gaze locked with hers.

The heat rose in her cheeks and she turned away and picked up a towel. "I'll get some of the bubbles off this lot. When you go down for the crib, dig out some clothes for them. I left the crates in the living room and then we'll get these children dressed and fed, including that poor bub."

She helped the children out of the bath one by one into the waiting towels. A pang of sadness pierced her chest as she looked down at the four shiny clean faces looking up at her expectantly. Her biological clock had gone past the ticking stage, it was ringing an alarm, but she'd never met anyone she wanted to have a family with.

She kneeled beside the children and pointed first to Madeleine.

"Now I know Maddy . . . is it okay if I call you that?"

A shy nod came in reply.

"And I know this is Billy. I need to know three more names and we're done." She rocked back on her feet with a smile and waited for the answer, but she was met with dead silence.

Tipping her head to the side, she pointed to the first twin and then turned her palms upward. "Do I have to guess?"

"Yep . . . but you never will," said the twin on the left.

"Come on then, we'll go down and get you dressed and if I haven't guessed by the time dinner is ready, you'll have to tell me." She looked seriously at the twins and held out one hand to each of them. "Deal?"

Two little hands shook hers vigorously.

Twenty minutes later, with Blake's assistance and after much giggling and sharing of clothes, the four children were dressed in their pyjamas. Ana was still going through the alphabet unsuccessfully guessing names and was up to Thaddeus, much to the mirth of the twin boys.

"Uncle Blake, you are going to have to introduce me to these children," she said with a smile.

Blake pointed at the twins and screwed his face up. "Benjamin and Broderick but answer to Benny and Roddy." His face broke into a huge smile and Ana's heart skipped a beat as he held her gaze. "But I never know which is which, or rather who is who, so you'll have to work that out for yourself. The baby is Jake, and you already know Maddy and Billy."

Ana looked over at the small girl who was sitting in the large, upholstered chair in the living room, legs tucked under her and reading her book. Reaching out to Blake, she gripped his arm and inclined her head towards Maddy. Blake casually strolled over and sat on the edge of the chair next to his niece as tears welled in the little girl's eyes.

"What will happen to Daddy if his . . . if his plane fell out of the sky?" She gave a little hiccough and looked up earnestly.

Ana's throat tightened. Her business problems were nothing compared to the possibility these children may have lost their father. She looked across at Blake waiting for him to answer.

"We don't know if Daddy's plane even went up in the sky. Mummy sent a message before saying they think it is broken down at the camp and they are going through the forest to rescue them." Her chest filled with warmth as he hugged the little girl.

"Like Dora and Diego," said Billy.

The three little boys looked at him and only the noise of the game blaring from Billy's iPad broke the silence until Blake nodded and replied, "That's right, Billy. Like Dora and Diego."

What a wonderful father he would make.

At that moment, Blake looked up and smiled at her. Ana's heart sank. He still had that killer grin that used to curl her toes and it was like those ten years had never happened. She looked away. No way was she going to complicate matters by falling for him all over again. There was a lot of water under the bridge since then and she'd moved on.

Once they'd fed the children and put them to bed, she'd tell him why she was here and then make another appointment to see him later in the week.

Blake's phone rang and he jumped up to get it from the table.

"Oh, hi, Mike. No, he didn't show. No message either." He glanced at Ana and mouthed an apology before continuing with the call. "Look, I can't talk at the moment, I have a bit of a family situation."

The heat rushed to Ana's face as she realised Blake was talking about her appointment. He obviously still hadn't realised what she'd said in the melee of noise and children.

"No, Mike, I'm not going to follow up. It doesn't matter anyway. I haven't even seen the figures for that side of the business. Something smells a bit off to me. The restoration department is definitely going to go."

Ana glanced at the children watching television and headed for the kitchen. She'd heard enough. Blake's voice followed her as she stood at the sink filling a glass with cold water.

Money . . . profit . . . mergers model . . . get rid of staff. The words confirmed her suspicions. He'd not changed a bit.

And he could still talk to his boss about all that while he was worried about his brother-in-law and taking care of five kids?

"Penny for your thoughts?" His quiet voice interrupted her brooding.

"I was thinking it's time to eat and then time for me to go home," she said tersely.

"It's Friday . . . it's pizza night," Billy claimed, as he walked into the kitchen behind his uncle.

Blake frowned at her before he reached out and took her hand between his. Her traitorous nerves tingled all the way to her shoulder.

"Where is home, Anastasia?" he asked quietly. "We will have to have a little talk after dinner, just you and me. We have a lot to catch up on." He turned to the children with a grin. "But now, I'm going to order in some pizza."

"Yes, we do." She pulled her hand from his and bent down to Billy. "Let's go and play a game while Uncle Blake gets dinner."

I don't know if it will ever be the right time to talk. She squared her shoulders as she followed Billy to the living room, ignoring the curious glance Blake threw her way.

But I'll give it my best shot when the time is right.

***

Two hours later after the pizza had been demolished, Blake sat back in the family room off the kitchen, looking out at the dog whose nose was pressed up against the once-clean glass sliding door. The sun had set, and the dog was whimpering.

"No way, boy. You're not coming into my house." The cleaning service would have their work cut out for them this week without adding dog hair to the mess.

The house had descended into chaos. Toys were strewn around the room; milk had been spilled on his sofa and he'd spent the last ten minutes retrieving pizza crusts from the floor.

Ana came in from the kitchen, untying the large apron he'd found in a drawer for her. "Remember the old dog we had in the house for a while?" Her face lit up in a wicked grin and he tried to ignore the ache that tugged at the sensitive parts of his body. "He used to eat all the food scraps."

"*You* had the dog, not we." He remembered it well. Ana had found a stray on the way home from the coffee shop one afternoon and the smelly mutt had lived in her room for a few days before Blake had caught her sneaking it out to the garden one night. "And I also remember it didn't stay very long." Blake knew his voice was short, but he couldn't cope with the chaos in front of him and deal with memories from the past at the same time.

45

"I lost that argument, didn't I?" Ana turned away from him and threw the apron untidily over the back of the sofa. "If you let the dog in, he'll clean up this mess in seconds." His mouth tightened as the apron slipped to the floor and she seemed blissfully unaware of the growing mess. "No way. I hate animals inside," he said. "There has to be a broom or something around here."

"So you're going to make that poor dog stay outside in the cold all night?"

"Of course, it's staying outside. There's already drool in the car and it's bad enough that the kittens are inside."

A strange feeling ran through him as Ana shook her head. It was though he was being judged and found wanting.

"He's a he, not an 'it'. Animals have feelings just like us you know." She went over to the window, and a trail of drool slid down the glass as the dog moved across to the window where Ana was standing. "He looks all lonely out there."

Maddy looked up from her book. "He'll have to come inside. Mummy got him so he made sure Billy stayed safe."

"I'll make sure Billy is safe and besides it's . . . I mean his . . . claws would scratch the floor," Blake said firmly. It was his house, and he would make sure the children stayed safe.

Ana reached over the back of the sofa and tugged the blanket around Billy's feet. "And that would be the end of the world... for you anyway, Blake."

##

Having Ana in his house was surreal. She'd stepped in to help without a second thought and it was like the old days again. But with five children thrown in. They'd barely had time to exchange more than a few sentences. And most of hers reeked with disapproval, but Blake tried to ignore the uncomfortable feeling that held him.

He'd spent time with the kids, but he didn't know they were so demanding. Jeannie seemed to take it all in her stride with no obvious effort.

"The house looks way more welcoming with a bit of mess." Ana tipped her head to the side and watched him as he searched for a broom. "Looks almost like the old share house days. You'd have a fit if you saw my cottage."

"I'd love to come visit you." At last she'd opened up a little.

Ana laughed and shook her head. "Trust me, Blake. You wouldn't cope."

Her face was alight with amusement and he knew she'd been teasing him about the dog. Somehow, she'd always known how to push his buttons. And he had to admit even though his house was a mess tonight, it wasn't really that bad.

The smell of pizza wafting through the living room mixed with the clean, soapy smell of the children curled up on the soft chairs overlaid the air fresheners in the power outlets low on the wall. Benny and Roddy were asleep already, curled up head to head with their legs entwined. Maddy's eyelids were drooping as she snuggled back into the chair, both kittens nestled in her lap. Blake smiled as her hand caressed their backs in her half-asleep state. Only Billy was wide awake, engrossed in a game on his iPad.

"I think it's time to put that away and get some sleep, Billy," he said quietly. "Time for bed, hey buddy?"

"No."

Anastasia smiled down at him and put her finger to her lips. "Leave him. It's only seven o'clock."

Blake held her gaze for a long moment and smiled at her. She'd gone quiet on him for a while before dinner, but now she seemed more relaxed. He knew nothing about her life now, but she certainly knew what to do to help him.

"Do you have children, Ana?"

"No. I've had no time for that. I have a career." She chewed on her lip as she looked back at him and she seemed preoccupied.

"I'm going to check on Jake. He was still asleep, last time I went up. You really do have the touch, Blake. His clothes were all on the right way. After that I'll get going."

Panic filled him at the thought of being left alone with the children. He sat back in his chair and sipped on a can of Coke. He'd foregone the glass of red wine he had been looking forward to since he wanted his full wits about him with a houseful of nephews, a niece, dog, cats and fish.

"Oh, damn," he said and jumped out of the chair. He hadn't fed the dog, who was still peering in through the double glass door.

"Billy, what's your dog's name?" he asked as he walked past his nephew and ruffled his hair.

"Jaws," Billy replied without lifting his eyes or fingers from the iPad.

Stepping out the back porch, he turned the light on and groaned. Jaws was aptly named. Anything that was not secured to the ground or a part of the greenery had been chewed into bits and now the stupid mutt had the nerve to lick his hand and look up at him with soulful brown eyes.

"I guess it's my fault. I should have fed you earlier." Blake pointed at the mess and spoke in a stern voice. "Did you do that? Just one more reason why you belong outside."

Jaws slunk away, tail between his legs while Blake filled the food bowl with some of the dog kibble Jeannie had packed.

Bless her, he thought, she'd even remembered to pack fish food in her hurry to leave for the airport. God, he hoped Rod was okay. A hollow ache settled in his chest. He knew the wilderness up there around the lodge. If the plane had gone down, it could be days before they found it. He wished he could be up there too, helping in the search, but he was needed here.

He thought his career was busy and used all his powers of creative thinking. But tonight he discovered that was nothing compared to feeding, bathing, and caring for five children and assorted pets.

He looked out over the twinkling lights of the canal. If he leaned across to the far edge of the porch, he could just see where the river joined the ocean.

The cedar door leading out to the balcony creaked and the musky fragrance of Anastasia's perfume wafted across to him. He turned and held out his hand, but she ignored it and moved to the other side of the post he was leaning against.

"Jake is still asleep," she said softly. "He stirred a little, but I patted him and he went straight back off." She laughed. "He's out like a light."

Blake didn't answer immediately, surprised by the relief that coursed through him. He stood there trying to think of the best way to ask her to stay longer. There was no way he could cope with this by himself. Having her close by felt so natural and they had eased into a comfortable truce, despite the way they'd left things years ago. He tried to block out the way she had disappeared so suddenly since Ana didn't seem inclined to discuss it.

"Is there anyone you have to go home to?" He waited for her to answer, his stomach clenching as he waited for her to say there was. With her looks and sweet personality, he would be very surprised if she didn't have a partner. They'd argued incessantly when they shared the house, but he hadn't realised how much she'd meant to him until she'd left

But no matter what her situation was, things had never been resolved between them and now he was about to call on her good nature again.

"No," she said slowly. "I live alone."

His mind whirled and his fingers itched to do a high five.

She was still single? Things were looking up.

"Will you stay the night?" He blurted it out and closed his eyes realising what he'd just asked.

"Look, I don't mean that like it sounded." He reached over and took her hand, surprised by the tension in her body. "I hoped you could help me with the children overnight. I know it's not your responsibility and I know we haven't had a chance to talk. But I just want to tell you how happy I am that you sought me out and came to visit. Once we get the kids to bed, we can do some catching up.

She opened her mouth to reply but he interrupted her before she could speak.

"Honestly, Anastasia. I can't do this alone. I can run a corporation, but this situation has got me terrified. There's no one else I can call on such short notice."

She stood there looking uneasy but didn't reply and he wondered whether she was thinking about that last night they'd spent together.

"Look, I know I must have upset you somehow that last night—"

She shook her head. "No, it's got nothing to do with that. Look, I've been trying to find the right time to tell you why I'm here –"

Before she could finish, Blake's mobile pinged on the kitchen counter. He hurried inside, to read the message then ran back out to the porch to Ana.

"Fantastic news. They've found the plane and they're all okay. Jeannie is still in Cairns but she's flying out to the lodge. Apparently, the plane bucked on the runway when they were taking off. Rod has a broken leg and that's the worst of it."

"Thank God." She came over and hugged him. He put his arms around her, and her soft hair brushed against his lips. He closed his eyes as that familiar fragrance took him back ten years.

"It's a relief. The kids'll be gone, and I can concentrate on business," he said.

Disappointment filled him as Ana stiffened and dropped her arms.

"I'll help you out tonight, but I'll have to leave first thing in the morning. I've got Sunday off, so I can come back tomorrow night and help you out for one more day if you really need me to." She looked up at him, biting her lip. Her brow was creased, and she ran her hand through her hair. "If Jeannie isn't back by then you'll have to make other arrangements, because that's all I can do, Blake."

"Can you leave me your mobile number . . . just in case I have an emergency?" he asked.

She went into the kitchen and wrote it on the small message board on the wall next to the fridge. The overhead light reflected on her silver-blonde hair and he had an urge to run his fingers through the soft strands.

She came back out on the porch with an expression that was almost sad. "Happy, now?" She looked up at him "I thought turning into an important businessman would have taught you how to keep a poker face. I won't run away again, Blake." He gave in to his desire and reached out for her, but she stepped back.

Confusion filled him as he watched her walk into the house. Maybe he was moving too quickly. She'd withdrawn into herself and he didn't have a clue what he'd done to cause it.

***

Ana showered quickly and dressed in the guest bathroom downstairs, pulling on the long T-shirt Blake had found for her. She put the soft white cotton up to her nose and inhaled the clean soapy smell of his shirt. She knew it had been freshly laundered, but she kidded herself that she could still smell Blake's masculine aroma in the soft fibres.

She tugged the T-shirt down as far as it would go and then returned to the family room. The children were all asleep on the soft chairs, including Billy, who had his iPad tucked under his knees. They'd decided to leave them there and not risk disturbing them while they were sleeping.

"Poor little things," she said. "It'll be so good to let them know their daddy is okay when they wake up."

Blake was curled up in a recliner, watching over them with a football game turned low in the background. "So you're a football fan now?" She tugged self-consciously at the T-shirt as he turned to face her.

Her stomach fluttered as he held her gaze before he replied with a laugh. "What choice did I have? I got hooked into watching it because that was all that was on the TV when you lived in the share house."

"I don't remember you watching it. You never used to come to the games with us."

"You were just focused on your beloved Broncos." His eyes didn't leave hers. "When you weren't watching the game, you were doing your cheer leader routine around the living room."

Ana had forgotten about the silly things she'd done in the share house days. Life had become too serious too quickly when Mum's condition had deteriorated. "Do you want a coffee or anything before I go upstairs? I have to go to the kitchen to make up a couple of bottles." She laughed nervously. "Jake's bound to wake up soon and he's going to be starving when he does."

"Yes, please." He didn't take his gaze off her and she turned into the kitchen as the heat ran up her neck.

"Still lots of cream and one sugar?"

His laugh followed her. "Black, no cream. Watching the arteries. I spend too much time at a desk these days."

She carried a tray back out with his coffee, along with two baby bottles in a warmer, ready for when Jake woke up, and a cup of peppermint tea for herself. She handed him his coffee.

"Still drinking the hippy stuff?" Blake gestured to her cup.

"I was pleased to see it in your cupboard," she replied.

"Habit." He shrugged. "Jeannie's started drinking it so now I always keep it on hand.

Ana picked up the tray and walked to the door, pausing before she headed for the stairs. For a moment, she considered raising the real reason she was here before she went up to the baby. But when she looked across at Blake, he'd dropped his head into his hands. He'd done that in college when he was stressed. Worry was etched into his forehead and he closed his eyes. It would have been wonderful, if she could have gone over to him and held him to comfort him.

Don't go there. Not the right time. For talk or comfort.

"I'll look after Jake through the night."

He lifted his head, and his forehead cleared as he smiled at her. "Good night, Ana. And . . .

thanks. I really appreciate it. I'm sure this was the last thing you expected when you called in."

She walked slowly up the stairs, reluctant to leave him alone, but Jake would be awake soon and besides, she was here for business, nothing more, and she had to put her old feelings aside. Blake had the same effect on her as he had all those years ago and she didn't like that one bit. Playing happy families and looking after the kids had brought them together quickly, but she knew it was a false scenario. She *had* to talk to him about the business before the end of the week. And as soon as she raised the issues she had with the takeover, Ana just knew they would have a raging argument. Her business philosophies had firmed over the years just as Blake's had. She'd read the interview in the newspaper with dismay. He was harder now in his attitude than he had been when they'd argued back at uni. And she'd heard his response to his boss on the phone earlier.

Maybe it would be easier if she just left the store before he even knew that she was one of his employees.

No.

She stiffened her spine.

Don't go there.

She was here to convince Blake there *was* a place for a restoration department in the new store. It was needed in Maleny, no matter how modern he wanted the store to be or how much money he wanted to make for his company.

The baby's cry was a blessed interruption to her thoughts, and she hurried into the spare bedroom with a bottle. She bent down to scoop little Jake out of the portable cot and laid him down on the bed to change his nappy.

Five minutes later, she was sitting in the alcove of the bay window, with a clean, sweet smelling baby sucking contentedly on a bottle.

Nothing to it.

She gazed out over the canal and mulled over her dilemma once more, her eyelids getting heavy, as she snuggled the baby to her chest. She shut her eyes just for a brief moment . . .

***

Blake turned the television off and leaned over each sleeping child, tucking them under their light blankets. It was a mild night but he had left the air conditioning on low so the house would stay warm. He lifted the kittens off Maddy's lap and took them into the kitchen for a saucer of milk, before checking on the disgraced dog that was now curled up on a seat on the back landing. Now that he'd been fed, he'd stopped chewing everything in sight.

Although Blake thought as he looked around the demolished garden, there was nothing much left for the dog to chew. He picked up a garbage bag from the laundry room and wandered around the small garden collecting half-chewed pieces of assorted sticks and garden tools. Cursing as he stubbed his toe on a broken stick, he gave up and left the rest of the mess for the morning. He locked the back door, checked his phone for messages and then walked quietly up the stairs to check on Anastasia and Jake.

That's all I'm doing. Just making sure they're okay.

Yeah, sure it is.

Admit it. You just want to look at her and be with her.

He'd met many women over the past ten years and had a couple of half-hearted relationships, but no one had ever fired that same spark Anastasia had lit in him.

Now he wanted to know all about her. Find out about her life, where she lived, what she did. If there was a chance of them renewing their friendship, he was not going to let her slip away this time. His work just didn't satisfy him anymore. Even the thought of another new store hadn't motivated him this time. He was more excited about his move back to the Sunshine Coast. Ana walking in from the street had given him lots to think about.

Once Blake set his mind on a path, there was no stopping him until he achieved his goal. That was the way he ran his businesses and Anastasia was now firmly in his sights.

He tapped lightly on the door of the guest bedroom, but there was no answer. He opened it and poked his head in. Jake was sound asleep in the crib but there was no sign of Ana. After checking the other bedrooms, concern rippled through him.

Jeez, man, that's what you get for indulging in daydreams. He ran quietly down the stairs, his mind working furiously.

Where the hell had she gone?

He unlocked the front door, heaving a sigh of relief when he saw the red BMW parked on the road. Resting his head against the door jamb, he took a deep breath in an attempt to calm down. He locked the door and set off on a search of the house from top to bottom. He was just checking the guest bathroom downstairs when Jake's loud cry came from upstairs. Taking the stairs two at a time, he ran along the top hall and pushed open the door of the guest bedroom where the empty cot had been. The cries got louder as he stood at the door and he could hear Ana's soft voice.

"It's okay, Jakey. Your Mummy will be back soon." There was silence for a moment and then a loud sucking sound filled the room. He tapped on the door and pushed it open. Anastasia was sitting in the bay window tucked into the large cushions and the swag curtains at the side half-obscured his view of her.

"Anastasia? Is everything okay?"

"Come in. He's just having his second bottle. I was in the bathroom when he woke up."

Blake looked down sheepishly and decided to be honest.

"What's wrong, Blake? Are the children okay?" Her voice rose and a worried expression crossed her face. "Is your brother-in-law okay?"

Staring at her, he pulled his hand though his hair and looked over her head through the window.

"I couldn't find you," he said quietly. "I thought you'd . . . left . . . again."

"And what about little Jake?" Her voice was sarcastic. "What did you think I was going to do with him? Leave him by himself and not tell you?"

"Of course not—"

"Well, we're fine up here. So you can go back down to the other children." Her voice was cold. "I'll be leaving at five a.m. I have to start work early and I need to go home and get changed first."

He couldn't help himself, reaching over and lifting her chin before he changed his mind. "Where's home, Anastasia?"

"None of your damned business and for the record, I go by Ana now. So you can either call me that or Ms. Delaney." She pulled her chin out of his grip and turned her head away. "Good night, Blake. Close the door on your way out."

Chapter Four

The house was quiet when Ana tried to slip out quietly without waking anyone, including Blake. She jumped when a warm hand grasped her elbow as she reached for the front door. She turned to face Blake; his hair was sleep-tousled and his eyes were bleary. Even half asleep, he still oozed sex appeal and her heart rate kicked when he touched her, his fingers sliding down to gently encircle her wrist.

"I'm sorry I thought the worst last night. You were such a great help." Blake reached over and tucked a loose strand of hair behind her ear and she pulled away from his touch. "I owe you big time. There's no way I could have done it alone."

Let me keep my job.

She pushed the thought from her mind and decided an apology was in order.

"I'm sorry for snapping at you." Ana stared at him ignoring the warmth that stayed on her cheek where his fingers had brushed her skin. "We were both tired and you had no idea why I had to leave last time. I would never have left you with the children without letting you know I'd gone. Last time I had no choice." Her voice shook and tears pricked the backs of her eyes as she remembered the grief that had consumed her on that morning ten years ago. Seeing Blake had brought it all back. "I'll be back in the late afternoon . . . that is . . . if you still think you need me?"

"Oh yes, please. If it wasn't for the baby, I could probably manage but—"

"I'll be back," she interrupted. "Now, I'm late, so I'll see you this afternoon."

She reached down for the still-damp shoes and when she straightened, Blake slid his other arm around her waist and held her before she could pull away.

"Thank you," he said softly. "I'm not going to let you get away so easily this time."

Ana tried to step back but he held her close, and a tremble ran through her as she looked up and saw the intent in his eyes. Her eyes stayed fixed on his as he slowly lowered his lips to hers and claimed her mouth in a gentle kiss.

For a moment, she closed her eyes and gave in to the feelings surging through her before she pulled back with a jerky movement.

What the hell am I doing?

"And that's a promise. Once things settle down, I'd like to renew our . . . acquaintance. I missed you, Ana.' Blake smiled down at her. "What are you working on today?"

"Just going to do my job. I have had a pretty boring life, Blake. I've stayed around here. Nothing like you. Cairns, Melbourne, Singapore." Heat surged into her cheeks as she realised she'd let slip that she'd kept tabs on his life. "Or at least that's what one of the papers said last week." She quickly covered her slip.softly

Ana ran down the stairs and opened the gate and didn't look back at him until she was safely in her car away from his touch. He waved and turned back into the house.

##

Ana pressed down hard on the accelerator after she turned onto the Sunshine Motorway. The feel of Blake's lips lingered on hers and she brushed her mouth with the back of her knuckles.

Why did he have to kiss me?

She'd left the house before it was light and, now that the sun had risen, she'd decided to take the coastal route home. She was heading off to a job later in the morning and had more time than she'd let on to Blake—she'd just needed to get out of the house before she blurted out to him why she was there. She needed to think more about how she was going to approach the discussion about the takeover now that they'd renewed their acquaintance on a more personal level. It was nothing like the meeting she'd planned.

Thirty minutes later, Ana cursed as she came upon roadwork at Mooloolaba. The M1 would have been the better choice but she'd needed the scenery and salt air to help clear her head. Longing for a coffee, she pulled to a stop to settle in for a lengthy wait. Closing her eyes for a moment, she put her fingers up to her lips and took a deep breath trying to block Blake—and that brief kiss—from her thoughts. Their current restoration job had to be finished up today and the last of the fine plaster work would take all of her concentration.

Ha, she thought. *You've got no chance.*

Her reaction to him was based purely on the memory of that one night and it was well known that a girl held a soft spot for her first lover.

That's all it is.

The fact that he was going to close down her department was much more complicated than any old feelings that may resurface. That was the big problem and the one she had to deal with first.

##

"Sienna, this moulding is perfect." Ana climbed down from the stepladder and tucked her hair behind her ear.

"Yes, I knew it would be as soon as I saw it at the store." Sienna stood back and surveyed Ana's work. "Just as well the Bennetts were happy to pay the extra. You're done and it looks great." She turned and pointed to the balcony that ran off the huge living room they were working in. "Georgie's got the coffee ready. You've got time for one now."

Ana had avoided taking a break all day because she knew the girls would be keen to know how her meeting with Blake had turned out. Working had been a convenient excuse since they'd already run over the contracted deadline for the job and promised the owners they'd be finished today. Reluctantly she pulled off her work gloves and removed her cap, shaking the rest of her hair free. No matter how hard she tried, she always managed to get plaster bits stuck in her hair.

The aroma of the much needed coffee drew her over to the worktable where her two best friends sat on upturned buckets on the balcony. The view over the ocean was spectacular as the morning sun dispersed the last fingers of sea mist lingering over the silvery surface of the water.

Sienna couldn't sit still and was trimming a piece of plaster. Georgie sat with her chin propped in her hand, her auburn curls tumbling down her shoulders as she stared out through the French doors at the ocean.

"Looks like the weather's turned for the better. That was a good storm we had yesterday." Ana closed her eyes and savoured the coffee. Wherever they worked, Georgie carried her coffeemaker and provided them with the best coffee. They were a great team and there was no way she was going to let it end just because a corporation had bought the store out.

"Forget the weather, Ana. Tell us what happened. Are we unemployed?" Sienna tapped her foot impatiently on the tiles that they had installed on the balcony a couple of weeks earlier and stared at her. "How much longer are you going to keep us hanging here?"

Ana looked away from Sienna and followed Georgie's gaze out over the ocean.

"Okay, girls, you've both have been so patient all morning and you've worked so hard to get this place finished. Once we pack up the gear, the store can bill this one out." Ana sighed and looked around the house. "I'll be sorry to leave this job. It's one of the best we've had."

Sienna stood and came around to where Ana was perched on the upturned bucket.

She placed her hands on Ana's shoulders and stood there until Ana looked up at her. Sienna's hair was black and cropped short in a pixie cut. Even though they were in work clothes, her face was beautifully made up, and a bright scarf fell softly from her shoulders over her work T-shirt. But there was nothing soft about her gaze.

"Ana, spill. What the hell happened?" She stepped back and folded her arms, staring hard at

Ana. Georgie turned away from looking at the ocean and sat back with an expectant look.

"Well . . . I don't exactly know yet," Ana replied slowly.

"What did he say? Is he likely to change his mind?" Sienna was persistent.

"I didn't exactly . . . er . . . get to tell him."

"Jeez, Ana. You're always too nice." Sienna tapped her hands on her arms and frowned. "What happened?"

Ana picked up her spoon and drew patterns in the fine plaster dust on the table. "That's why I don't want to go into business ourselves. You both know I'm no good at dealing with people. I'd much rather just do the work."

"There's something not quite right here." Georgie spoke for the first time and her voice was soft.

Georgie knew her all too well. She was intuitive and sensitive to feelings, whereas Sienna would crash over anyone who stood in her way. All Georgie wanted was a house and family of her own and she'd been looking for Mr. Right for years. Ana smiled as she thought of the number of times they'd heard Georgie say 'he's the one,' only to pick herself up and move on again when she was disappointed.

"I didn't get a chance to talk about the store and our work. I'm going back there to see him again tonight."

"Jeez, don't tell me Mr. Big Shot made a move on you?" Georgie's face lit up in an interested grin. "Is he a hunk? Did you go out for dinner?"

"He had a bit of a family emergency and I helped him out, that's all."

Sienna rolled her eyes. "And knowing you, Ana, you wouldn't have brought up any business to rock the boat." She stood up and gathered the cups. "I'm coming back with you tonight. Our jobs are at stake here, girlfriend, and you need to toughen up."

Ana stood next to Sienna and kept her voice firm. "No. I'll handle it. Trust me. I know what's at stake." She turned and gestured to the tools and plaster buckets lying around. "Now if we don't get this mess cleaned up, we won't have a job to fight for. Oh, and Sienna?" She grinned as Sienna frowned at her. "Can I borrow your car again? You were right, it's much faster than mine."

Sienna and Georgie packed up the worktable and tools, and carried them out to Ana's ute, loading it up while she wiped the floor to remove the last of the plaster dust. Her phone beeped in her pocket and she smiled as she pulled it out and read the short message.

Be quick. Bring food and iPad charger.

Sounded like Mr. Hot Shot CEO needed help . . . and fast.

***

Blake held Jake tucked under one arm as he tripped over a kitten and then bumped his hip on a table that shouldn't have been in his path. The twins had spent the afternoon sliding down the hallway in their socks and it had been easier to move the table out of harm's way, rather than getting them to stop. Billy had been sitting upside down on the corner of the sofa drumming his heels against the wall and squealing since his iPad had run out of charge hours ago.

Well, it'd seemed like hours.

Blake had turned the damn house upside down looking for the charger— it seemed to be the only thing Jeannie had forgotten to pack. Toys, clothes, and half-chewed cookies covered the floor from the foyer to the kitchen. His house was starting to look very different.

And the smell.

Blake headed for the bathroom to do something about the revolting mess that was in Jake's nappy, praying that Ana was on her way.

"Maddy, if Anastasia comes to the door, can you please let her in? But no one else, okay?"

"Okay, Uncle Blake."

At least the twins were watching cartoons on the Disney channel. *The Octonauts and Baby Shark* had kept them entertained on and off all day—over and over and over— and he'd barely had time for even a twinge of guilt about the junk food he'd fed them. One day of biscuits and chips wouldn't stunt their growth, surely? Thank God Ana was going to be here soon to help him out He had tried calling every nanny service in the area, but it seemed you had to book weeks ahead for five kids.

He had to be at the store on Friday to do the handover. Surely Jeannie would be back by then. Mike was coming up from Melbourne and it was a huge deal.

Oh shit, he was supposed to be having dinner with him tomorrow night.

He ran a shallow bath and turned his head away as he stripped the baby down.

As he scrubbed Jake, Blake thought of Anastasia . . . or Ana if that's what she wanted to be called now. He owed her so much for helping him.

He was pleased she had sought him out. Even though he was the one who'd put their friendship at risk that night years ago, when he'd first kissed her, he'd been the one who got hurt when she'd ditched him the next morning. But last night the spark had rekindled between them and he hoped she was feeling it too.

Why did she come and see me?

Was it to do with his money or just for old time's sake? She looked like she'd done okay in whatever her career was. The suit and the BMW pointed to success, and she'd said she was single so there wasn't a wealthy husband in the background.

Maybe a divorce settlement?

And he'd kissed her before his brain had kicked into gear. He needed to find out all about her before he got sucked in.

"Come on, little guy. We'll get you dried off, dressed and fed and then you can fill that diaper again."

He lifted the slippery child out of the soap suds and grinned. Maybe he could get the hang of this kid thing.

***

All the way to the coast, Ana practised her pitch to Blake but any thoughts of speaking to him tonight about job security for their team disappeared when she stepped from the car. Muted screaming drifted out through the open windows. She grabbed the grocery bags, hitched her small backpack onto her shoulders, and headed quickly through the gate. The closer she got, the louder the cries became, and she realised it wasn't the baby. Her well-rehearsed speech and business plans fled from her mind as she moved the bags to one hand and pushed the buzzer.

She waited for a couple of minutes before she pounded on the door.

Eventually a quiet little voice came from the other side. "Who is it?"

"It's Ana. Let me in, Maddy."

"No, Uncle Blake said only Anastasia." The little girl's voice was firm. "What's the password?"

"What password? Where's Uncle Blake?"

"The password to get into the castle."

"Is Uncle Blake there? And who's crying?"

"Uncle Blake is up in the bathroom and Billy is crying."

"Can you please let me in? I am Anastasia." Ana put the bags down. She could see Maddy's silhouette through the opaque glass. "Why is Billy crying?"

"You're not Anastasia, you said you were Ana. And Billy's crying 'cause he's hurting."

Visions of blood and cut fingers filled her mind. If Blake was upstairs, the children could have gotten into anything. Every childhood accident she'd ever read about, kids putting cutlery into power outlets and getting into kitchen knife blocks flashed through her mind. God, what about all the poisonous detergents and stuff in the cupboards? They hadn't even thought about childproofing his house.

"Maddy, you have to let me in. Where is Billy hurting?"

"What's the password?" Maddy repeated.

The door stayed firmly closed.

Ana pulled out her phone and scrolled through her contacts before she recalled she never asked Blake for his number. Then she remembered the text he'd sent earlier today, opened the message and pressed call.

The little figure disappeared from the other side of the glass. "Uncle Blake, your phone's ringing," Maddy called out.

Ana leaned against the door as Blake answered.

Thank God.

"Hello? Anast—I mean Ana. How long till—"

"Blake I'm at the door and I can't get in without a password."

"What . . . oh . . . okay, I'm on my way down."

It was only seconds before Blake appeared through the glass and opened the door. He stood there with a dripping wet and naked baby in his arms. She shoved past him, leaving the bags on the porch. His hair was tousled, and his T-shirt was soaking wet, but he was still smiling despite the screams coming from the living room.

"Is Billy hurt?" she asked urgently as she ran through the door.

Maddy was sitting primly on the sofa reading a book and didn't look up as Ana flew past, following the noisy cries to the large white sofa in the corner of the room. She kneeled down and glanced back at Blake who was close behind her.

"It's all right," he said hitching Jake up onto his shoulder. His wet T-shirt was plastered to the well-defined muscles on his chest and she was upset with herself for noticing, despite her concern for Billy. "He's not hurt," Blake reassured her.

The little boy was in the corner with a blanket over his head. Ana reached in gingerly and lifted it. The cries subsided for a moment and a tear-streaked little face looked back at her.

"Did you bring the iPad plug?" he asked.

She nodded and he smiled, before pulling the blanket back over his head. "Go and plug it in now and fix the fire fish," he said. "Please."

Ana stood up slowly and turned to Blake. The expression on his face was priceless. Both the suave businessman looks, and the sexily tousled man of this morning had been replaced with a harried face decorated with a blob of ketchup or something red above his right eye, and if she wasn't mistaken that was baby poop down the front of his T-shirt.

"Welcome to my day," he said as she fought the laughter bubbling up from her chest.

***

Blake watched as Ana pulled the iPad charger out of the large bag, led Billy over to the power outlet, and plugged it in. Billy sat down as though to settle in and watch it charge. His admiration for Ana grew as she took the little boy's hand and led him over to the twins and whispered quietly in his ear. He climbed happily onto the sofa.

She was casually dressed in a pair of loose cotton pants and a cropped T-shirt which hugged her small, high breasts, and her hair was pulled back into a high ponytail. She looked like a teenager, more like the Anastasia he'd known ten years ago. Her slim body was toned, and he wondered if she worked out to keep herself fit. He knew nothing about her life now and wanted to know all about her. Needed to know. What she did, where she lived and if they could be . . . friends again.

At least friends. The last ten years had passed so quickly, but damn it, he was fascinated by her. It was as though his life in that time, had disappeared in a puff of smoke.

She cleared her throat and he realised he'd been caught staring at her. His cheeks heated and he quickly thought of a way to cover up his wandering thoughts.

"How did you persuade him to watch television?" He inclined his head to Billy, now happily snuggled between his two older siblings.

"I said I'd fix the fire fish on the iPad."

"The what?"

"Do you think he is on the computer a little too much? Or are we just spoiling him because of the situation?" Ana frowned and twirled her fingers through her ponytail. "Anyway, the fire fish is 'wireless'. He wants me to turn the wireless on. He showed me the settings folder and it needs a password! Can you believe it? How old is he? Four?"

Blake looked over at his nephew whose eyelids were now getting heavy. He had made a fort out of the sofa cushions and only his little head was visible. A surge of love rushed through his chest and he turned to Ana.

"Billy is special...or to put it in the right terminology—he's on the autism spectrum. He has the iPad for speech therapy and learning his letters, but I think we are getting conned a bit because I know there are rules about when he can play games and I'm pretty sure Jeannie leaves the Wi Fi turned off."

Ana looked back at him and wrinkled her nose and he wondered what she was going to say. She had handled Billy so well. Come to think of it, all five children had responded to her gentle, caring way. Surely, she wasn't intimidated now that she knew Billy had special needs. But a slow smile spread across her face and he waited for her to speak.

"Blake, do you know you have baby poop all over your shirt?"

"Oh, Jeez." He looked down and pulled the shirt over his head, taking care to hold the offending piece of fabric well away from his face. He turned to her and this time it was him that caught her checking *him* out. Or rather checking his abs out.

"I'm going for a shower, want to come and wash my back?" He kept his voice light as he teased her.

She lifted her head and held his gaze.

"Maddy can cook dinner. You go and start, and I'll be up in a moment," she deadpanned.

For one brief moment his heart skittered and then he burst out laughing.

"Still got your sense of humour, I see, Anast—Ana."

"It's okay, I'll answer to either. Call me whatever suits you." She smiled at him and headed for the family room. He stood for a moment, watching her as she entered into some serious negotiations with the boys about eating vegetables for dinner. It was going to be a very interesting weekend.

Chapter Five

"No, no, no." Billy slipped down from the chair and crawled beneath the table. Ana bit back a smile as Blake ran his hand through his hair. It had been sexily mussed since the children had arrived, and the neat and well-dressed businessman had been replaced by a harried uncle in jeans and a stained T-shirt. He was looking even more casual than he had back in their college days.

Billy had spent the first half of the meal refusing to eat, until Maddy pointed out that his vegetables were in the wrong order. As Roddy and Benny scarfed down their dinner to get to their dessert, Ana had rearranged Billy's vegetables until she'd hit on the right sequence of colours.

"Orange, white, orange, green." Ana turned to Blake. "You'd better write that down."

After dinner, they'd bathed the children together and Jake had obliged by going to sleep without any fuss.

Blake had grinned at her as a squirt from Benny's water pistol had soaked her shirt.

"At least I have a change of clothes with me tonight," she said. Then heat surged into her cheeks as she realised the clear outline of her nipples was visible through the wet cotton and Blake was taking in the view.

Ana folded her arms across her chest and frowned at him. "It's your turn to dry and dress them tonight."

"Spoilsport." Blake held her gaze and Ana was the first to look away.

Once they were dressed, the children settled in to watch *Octonauts*—again—and Jake woke for a quick feed. Ana tidied up the kitchen after she gave him the bottle, and Blake wandered in from the family room. He sat on a stool at the breakfast bar and Ana concentrated on rinsing the dishcloth, aware of him watching her, until he laid his head on his crossed forearms on the counter.

"You look exhausted." She wiped down the kitchen sink one last time and hung the cloth over the faucet. "I'll finish up here."

"I am," he said. "I don't know how Jeannie does it by herself. Rod spends a lot of time travelling to farms out in the western district, and she runs a web design business from home, too." Blake lifted his head from his arms and smothered a yawn.

"Superwoman," Ana replied. "How about a coffee?"

"Great. Now that it's finally quiet . . . and tidy—" Blake grinned at her and something tugged in her lower belly— "we can finally catch up. You can tell me all about your life."

"I'd probably bore you to tears. Not a lot to tell. I didn't finish uni and I stayed in my hometown."

He glanced at her with a frown. "You were never boring. Besides you need to tell me why you had that appointment with me yesterday?"

Ana gestured around the room and changed the subject ignoring his question. When they sat down with their coffee, she would come clean and tell him why she was here. "Did I tell you how much I love your house?"

Ana looked away, pretending to examine the kitchen. Actually it was worth looking at and piqued her designer interest. Brightly coloured tiles edged the huge bay window which hung over the kitchen sink and looked out over the small balcony and garden edging the canal. If she leaned forward, she could just get a glimpse of the sky too.

"I had it built when I knew I was coming home." Blake had slipped silently from the stool and moved to stand next to her. Ana turned and his broad chest filled her vision. Her fingertips began to tingle as the urge to run her fingers over the smooth fabric, over his well-toned muscles filled her. She raised her hand and took a step back, but Blake followed her, his warm masculine aroma filling her senses.

He placed his hands gently on her shoulders and she held his gaze, warmth shooting low in her belly again as his lips turned up in a sexy smile.

Gradually the pressure of his fingers increased, and he pulled her closer to him.

"I'm back to stay, you know. I didn't know what I was missing out on until I came back home." He held her gaze and Ana gave in, lifting her hands to run her palms across his chest.

The warmth moved up to her chest when he drew in a quick breath as her fingers ran over the soft fabric.

"And now that we've reconnected there's even more incentive to stay here." His voice was husky, and she lowered her eyes to rest on his lips. Grasping his T-shirt between her fists she tried to fight the hunger that was overtaking her. She couldn't let this physical attraction to him get out of hand. Not until he knew the real reason for her visit. She had to convince him how valuable their business was to the store—and the community of Maleny— before anything could happen between them that would only complicate matters even more.

Her stomach churned at the thought even as his lips hovered above hers and her mind whirled in turmoil. Should she just blurt it all out?

"Oh and by the way, Blake . . . you hold my future and that of my two best friends in your hands."

If he ran a business the way he'd talked at university, the way she'd read in the papers, their jobs wouldn't matter a hoot to him if they stood in the way of profit. Even if she was sleeping with him.

"I stuck with all those ideas I had ten years ago." His warm breath puffed on her lips as his mouth moved closer to hers.

"What?" Ana squawked out the single word and tipped her head back and looked up at him as his eyes stayed locked on hers.

What was he, a mind reader?

"Building this house. It's what I used to imagine as the perfect house when we lived in that old house on the river at Toowong.'

"Oh, the house." She let go of the breath she'd been holding, and he looked down at her curiously.

"What did you think I was talking about?"

"Nothing." She stepped out of his arms and moved across to the coffeemaker, trying to steady her hands so he couldn't see how much his nearness threw her. "I found a job where I can make a difference in people's lives." She held the coffeepot under the tap. "And the community benefits from my work."

Blake moved back to the stool and she was conscious of his eyes on her as she sought the right words. Tangling with him on a sexual level was the last thing she'd expected when she'd driven here yesterday. The hard-headed businessman had morphed into the sexy man who now had his smouldering gaze locked on her. It was so hard to reconcile this Blake with the CEO of a company who was about to destroy not only her life, but that of the community as well.

But then the sexy smile turned to a cynical laugh. "Don't tell me you are still a soft touch for anyone who comes begging, Ana? Or have you become a social worker?"

Cold iced her veins and she welcomed the anger that filled her.

"Yes, Blake. I'm still a soft touch." She would not let her feelings take over what she had to say to him. "And I'm proud of it. I told you I was your four o'clock appointment yesterday, so you go figure that out." She switched the coffeemaker on and walked to the door trying to put as much distance between them as possible. "Once Jeannie's back, I'll make another appointment and we can have a business discussion without all this." She waved her hand in the air but almost gave in as his face filled with disappointment.

Remember, hard-headed businessman.

"I'm going to sit with the children for a while, and then I'm going to bed."

"Thanks for making the coffee." Blake's face closed and he nodded at her. "I'll see you in the morning."

The problems filling her mind kept Ana awake and finally she crept back out to the kitchen. All was quiet and dark, and she poured a coffee taking it outside onto the back porch before settling into the double swing. Jaws jumped up next to her and she smiled. She ran her fingers through his soft fur as he placed his head in her lap. He was simply one more example of how she and Blake were so different.

She leaned back and closed her eyes, trying to focus on the sounds of the night and to calm the thoughts scurrying around in her head. A soft shower of summer rain had just passed by and the muted croaking of frogs drifted up from the back of the garden. Ana sighed and leaned her head back.

There were so many different arguments she could use to try to convince Blake. Even though she'd seen a softer side to him as he cared for the children, she was sure the businessman wasn't far away. He had to be hard to do the sort of takeovers he did, where layoffs were a given and people lost their livelihoods.

Eventually she pushed Jaws gently off her lap and headed upstairs to bed. A little voice muttering caught her attention before she reached the top of the landing, and she turned toward the bedroom where the children were sleeping. She stood in the doorway, but the voice came from behind her in Blake's room. The door was wide open, and she stepped quietly to the entrance. Before she could tap on the door, the little voice muttered again, and she leaned forward to peek in.

Blake was sound asleep, the sheet covering him from his waist down. His arms were around Billy who was nestled into his uncle's chest with one little hand tightly gripping the fabric of Blake's T-shirt. As she watched, Billy muttered in his sleep again and she stepped back quickly out of sight as Blake made a soothing sound.

Ana's chest closed and she hitched a breath as tears pricked the back of her eyelids. Maybe, just maybe if Mum hadn't got sick, she and Blake may have made a life together and he could have been holding their child.

She knew she was reading too much into their one night together, but damn it, all the feelings she'd had for him ten years ago had come rushing back and overwhelmed her.

Brushing her eyes impatiently, she tiptoed back to the guest room, before looking down into the crib at baby Jake who was sleeping soundly. Slipping off her robe, she climbed into bed and shook her head. If anyone had told her a few days ago where she'd be tonight, she would have said they were crazy.

Maybe she was...and that was the reason she hadn't given all the details to Sienna and Georgie.

##

"Don't forget the spare nappies—and the wipes." Ana called out to Blake, and grinned at him as he hitched the baby bag onto his shoulder. His brow wrinkled in a frown. Despite the way they'd ended the night last night, he'd been friendly and pleasant to her this morning. It was as though they hadn't had that conversation in the kitchen. Maybe he was trying to ignore the physical attraction between them too?

"I'll never get used to this. How much stuff do kids need?" He let the bag drop to the floor, shoved Jake at Ana and ran up the stairs. "I forgot the wipes."

Jake gurgled happily in Ana's arms and she burrowed her face into his sweet-smelling, soft hair. It was a beautiful Sunday morning and Billy had informed them that Sunday was park day, so the children were dressed, and had their shoes on. They all stood in a row on the front porch, still for the first time since breakfast. Even Billy stood calmly while he sang "Incy Wincy Spider" to Maddy, who was doing the hand actions on his arm. Ana lifted her face from Jake's hair and smiled down at them. She remembered playing house with Sienna and Georgie when they were little, but real kids were very different than baby dolls.

They did things. They made noise. They created mess.

And they required constant supervision.

After Blake returned triumphantly with the baby wipes, they set off for Peninsula Park at the end of the street. Blake led their little group with Billy as he pushed Jake's stroller. She held each of the twins' hands as Maddy walked beside them.

Ana giggled and looked up at Blake as Jaws emitted another long, howl. "We really should have brought him. He'll drive the neighbours crazy."

"Five children aren't enough to worry about?" Blake walked on, seemingly unbothered by the dog's mournful cries that accompanied them along the street.

Billy tugged on her arm with his free hand.

"Why has that house got funny windows?" he asked pointing to the old building.

Ana looked up at the house they were passing. "They're made of coloured glass."

"But why has it got funny windows?" he repeated.

"It's called leadlight. Ask Uncle Blake." She inclined her head to Blake and smiled as they crossed the road.

By the time they crossed the next road and walked along the edge of the park, Billy had forgotten about the windows and was reciting the colours of the cars as they whizzed past. They stepped up on to the elevated footpath which edged the park and Ana herded the children across the grass to the swings. The boys ran around whooping and rolling on the grass, followed by Maddy who walked along at a more sedate pace.

Ana turned and spoke to Blake. "She's a serious child."

He unbuckled Jake's seatbelt, lifted the baby from the stroller and placed him into Ana's arms. Warmth filled her chest as the little boy reached up, grabbed her hair, and cooed happily. Blake smiled at her and the heat spread to her cheeks. She buried her face in the baby's hair to hide the flush.

"She takes the responsibility of being the eldest very seriously," Blake replied as he found a place to spread the rug on the grass. "Although she was always like that, even before the boys came along."

"Tell me about Jeannie." Ana decided to keep the conversation focused on Blake's family as she settled on the rug, not giving him the opportunity to ask her any probing questions.

Blake eased down onto the rug beside her and looked at her intently. "Jeannie and Rod moved back to Noosa when Maddy was born. One of the reasons I came back was because I missed being around the family."

Ana shifted her gaze from his and glanced around. They were surrounded by families enjoying the morning sunshine in the park and dog owners who were walking a variety of breeds along the paths. A few clouds were racing high above them and the wind was ruffling the water on the canal.

"What about you, Ana? You said you live alone? Where's home?"

"Uncle Blake, Uncle Blake!" Maddy's cry of distress drifted across to them before she could reply. "Billy's stuck."

Blake jumped up and ran across the short distance to the playground where Billy was hanging upside down, his knees curled over the top rung of the jungle gym and a huge grin spread across his face.

Ana settled on the rug with the baby lying on his back beside her and watched Blake reach up to Billy who was now at the top of the slide. Her heart lurched. Just looking at him brought all the feelings she'd managed to bury for all those years came flooding back in one huge wave. She closed her eyes and drew in a deep breath.

Wake up.

It had all been immature mooning over something she would never have. And they were so different, a relationship would never have worked between them. This was getting out of hand. In addition to the complications of those stupid lovesick memories intruding in her thoughts—and that's all they were, she told herself sternly—she had her own commitments to attend to.

Her promise to help out at the community markets on Sunday had already been broken and she'd had to arrange for Georgie to pick up Thelma and Mitzi, the two elderly ladies she drove to the markets each month with their baskets and crates full of handmade goods. Even though time had been short lately, she hated letting down the local folk and it had been bad luck that Blake had needed her help on the weekend of the community market.

She'd also promised Magda all the accounts would be up to date and ready to enter into the computer last Friday, but with the trip to Noosa, the rush back to Sunshine Coast to finish the Bennett job, and now another day helping Blake with the children, the three cardboard shoe boxes shoved full of invoices and receipts were still sitting on her kitchen table. She needed to get those accounts done now more than ever as a way to show Blake how profitable their department could be.

She had to convince Blake. She just *had* to. Helping him with the children might soften him up a little but she knew it was merely postponing the inevitable clash she knew their meeting would turn into. They'd argued so ferociously at uni over social issues, she just knew he would disagree with her and she would be hard pressed to hold back what she really thought about him destroying their little community business. This peaceful existence between them was not real. Once Blake knew why she was really here, they would clash as fiercely as they had before. They were just too different and caring for the children was one of the few things they had ever agreed on.

Ana groaned and Jake turned his wide blue eyes to her. Reaching down, she tickled him under his chin and was rewarded with a huge, gummy smile.

"Okay, Jake, I'll forget about all my worries and pay you some attention. Wise advice, young man. Thank you."

The excited calls of the children drifted across to her during a lull in the traffic noise. The twins were still on the swings, Maddy was patting a small, white dog, and Billy's arm was outstretched as he pointed to a small fountain at the edge of the canal.

"But I like to swim." His little voice became louder as Blake shook his head and pointed back to the jungle gym.

"I want to swim," Billy said insistently.

Blake lifted Billy back up onto the top of the slide and turned to watch the twins. As soon as the little boy landed in the soft sand at the bottom of the slide, his little legs pumped furiously as he took off.

"Blake!" Ana pointed to Billy as he charged past the gardens and through the gum trees towards the fountain. She jumped to her feet, picked up the baby and headed for the swings.

"I'll watch them while you get Billy," she called to Blake.

But by the time Blake caught up to Billy, the little boy had removed his shoes and socks, and stood in the middle of the fountain peeling off his pants. Blake walked around the fountain reaching out to Billy as he splashed around just out of his uncle's reach. As they disappeared behind the post in the middle, Maddy and the twins jumped off the swings and ran across to Ana.

"Billy's not allowed in the water because he can't swim. Daddy says." Maddy nodded her head. "But we won't tell him because if he has a sore leg, he might get mad."

The sound of a loud splash followed by a child's giggling reached them, just before a little figure appeared from the side closet to the road and took off across the grass toward the edge of the park and the busy traffic on Shorehaven Drive. Ana's heart lodged in her throat. The park area was raised above the street and was not fenced along the footpath. It was not a huge drop, but it was high enough for a small child to take a nasty fall. She was helpless, across on the other side of the grassed area, holding the baby and with three other children beside her. Blake took the shortest route to catch Billy—straight through the shallow fountain.

"Billy, stop. Billy!" Her shrill cry was muffled by a bus as it roared past.

"Stop," she screamed again, grasping the baby to her chest and running toward Billy. But the little boy kept running, down the sloping grassy hill toward the busy street.

Parents jumped to their feet, watching in horror as Billy reached the drop to the footpath and stood there beside the busy street, his little bare legs white in the bright sunshine.

"Billy! Freeze!" Maddy's imperious voice rang out over all the cries and traffic noise. Billy stopped and turned around, teetering on the edge of the concrete wall above the footpath. Blake pushed past Ana, water dripping from his hair and shirt, from when he'd leaned into the fountain to get Billy out. Kneeling down, he put his arms around the small boy. He looked up at Ana and the look on his face brought tears to her eyes. The love for his little nephew shone from his face and Ana's heart lodged in her throat.

To have Blake look at me like that . . .

He dropped his gaze as he held the small boy close to his chest.

"Do you like to swim too, *Unca* Blake?" His voice carried over to Ana as the little boy looked earnestly up at his uncle.

##

It was a slow and quiet walk back to Blake's house. The baby was sucking contentedly on a dummy in his stroller, the older children walked along holding Blake and Ana's hands, disappointed that the picnic lunch lay untouched in the basket they had packed. The only sound was the wet, squelching suck every time Blake took a step. His shoes were soaked, and his socks were wet. Billy's hand was firmly in his grasp and he had Blake's dry T-shirt around his shoulders. Ana kept her eyes off Blake's bare chest.

"No more trips to the park." His whisper was low, and Ana's heart went out to him. Blake hadn't let go of Billy since reaching him at the edge of the ledge above the sidewalk, and he'd kept his expression closed. She could imagine what was going through his mind and was sure she would have nightmares about Billy falling under a bus. They stopped at the busy intersection and Billy tried to pull away from Blake.

"Ow, let go."

Ana caught Blake's eye as she spoke to the small boy. "Do you want to have a turn holding my hand, Billy?"

Blake looked back at Ana and shook his head. "I've got him." His voice was clipped. The relaxed, carefree Blake had disappeared.

It was obvious he was in no mood to listen to her now which would only make her case harder to plead. She'd missed her chance last night by letting herself get angry with him. She would meet with him at the store when he turned up in Maleny. It would just have to wait.

***

As soon as they got inside, Ana took Billy upstairs for a bath and Blake switched the television on for the others. Then he walked the perimeter of the bottom floor, making sure every door and window was locked.

If there was one thing he couldn't handle, it was being out of control. Taking the children for a picnic in the park had proved disastrous. It should have been a . . . well . . . it should have been a walk in the park.

And he'd failed.

He closed his eyes. Never again did he want to feel as helpless as he had when Billy had teetered on the edge of the busy street. God, imagine if he'd had to call Jeannie and tell her Billy was hurt . . . or worse.

"Blake." Ana's voice was quiet and firm. "Billy's okay. Everyone's safe. Don't stress."

She settled Billy onto the sofa with the other children and spread the picnic rug on the floor in front of the television before laying out their food.

"Could you get me a cold drink, please?" she said.

Blake headed to the kitchen without a word. Like him, Ana had been preoccupied since they'd left the park and he could understand why. She'd taken on the responsibility of helping him with the kids without hesitation and he'd really taken advantage of her. He'd expected a lot asking her to help him just because she'd happened to come along at the right time. He wouldn't ask her for any more help after today. He would just have to cancel the dinner with Mike and Helen if Jeannie wasn't back in time. Ana came into the kitchen, slid onto the stool on the other side of the bench and took the large mug of coffee he pushed across the shiny granite top.

"Ana." Her hair was loose around her shoulders and she reached up and flicked it back from her face as clear blue eyes gazed back at him. An uneasy feeling lodged in his throat.

A wholesome face, no makeup and plain, simple clothes. She'd shed the business suit and looked so much like the Ana of old.

Very different to the corporate, elegant women he'd taken out over the years in Melbourne.

Which was the real Ana? There was still a mystery about her appearance on his doorstep and he'd let himself get side-tracked by her last night.

But damn it, I can't keep my hands off her.

Glancing at her hands as she lifted the coffee to her lips, he noticed her long fingers had short, clipped fingernails, and were free of any adornment and he wondered once more what had brought her to his doorstep.

He cleared his throat. "Look, I've been thinking. I'm going to call a nanny service again. I'm sure they'll be able to find someone right away if I pay enough."

Her face was closed, and she nodded without speaking. Turning away from him, she stared out the window and sipped her coffee.

"Are you okay?" He felt like a heel. She was probably just as shaken by Billy's near-miss as he was.

All was quiet in the room. The muffled sound of television cartoons drifted in from the living room and Ana slipped off the stool and moved across to the door.

She glanced in at the children before looking back at him.

She swallowed and lifted her chin.

"Blake, I need to tell you something."

Chapter Six

Ana focused her gaze on the second hand of the large French provincial wall clock above the doorway. She looked at the fancy metal whorls as she struggled to find the way to tell Blake why she was really here, and what she wanted from him. In the early hours of this morning, she'd had it all planned out, but now she figured she might as well just blurt it out instead of waiting any longer.

"Fire away." Blake's gaze was fixed on her and his serious expression made her heart thud even louder. Ana gripped the side of the stool until the cold chrome bit into the sides of her palms.

"I never expected to see you again." She swallowed and sought for the right words. "That is until I decided to come on Friday."

"Yes?" He tilted his head to the side, and she stared at him. Curious eyes looked back at her, but the smile crinkles were still there. He hadn't shaved this morning and sexy stubble covered his jaw. She closed her eyes and focused on her thoughts, instead of thinking of running her lips along his rough cheek.

"So I made the appointment to see you about the store—"

"What do you mean the store?" Blake's expression tightened and Ana's stomach rolled in anticipation of his reaction.

"Do you mean, *you* were my appointment? You were sent to do the pleading for the restoration guy from Maleny? Why not tell me straight up? Still wearing your heart on your sleeve, Ana?"

Angry words rose on Ana's tongue and she bit them back.

How dare he? How could she ever have thought that he'd softened? The ring of the doorbell interrupted them before she could reply, and Blake stared at her as he walked around the counter. "Wait here. I want to hear the rest and why this loser couldn't come himself. And why was it such a big secret? Not only can he not turn a profit, but he sends someone else to do his begging?"

Ana swivelled around on the stool and watched him as he strode across the living room. She clenched her fists on her lap as the anger burned up her throat.

I tried to tell him, and he didn't listen.

"No wonder the store was ready for a takeover." Blake's words came from the living room as he disappeared into the living room heading to the front door. His denim jeans hugged his butt nicely and she closed her eyes to block the sight, but his words stuck in her head, going round and round like a mantra. She was not interested in how sexy he looked. Forget the sexy, he was still as sexist as ever.

He didn't even consider for one minute I might be the restoration guy.

"Mummy, Mummy." The excited voices of the twins and Maddy interrupted her thoughts and she opened her eyes. Blake's sister crossed the room from the front landing and bent down and dropped a kiss on the heads of her children who had jumped up to greet her.

Ana's eyes pricked as Jeannie stopped and looked down at Billy who was sound asleep on the end of the sofa. She picked up the little hand hanging down by his side, tucked it into his chest, and ran her fingers softy down the side of his face.

Jeannie followed Blake into the kitchen and smiled at Ana.

"Anastasia, it's so lovely to see you again. I was in such a panic on Friday, I didn't even recognise you."

"It has been a long time, Jeannie." Their paths had crossed only occasionally in the year Ana had lived at the house, but Blake's older sister had always been friendly to her. "I can't believe these five beautiful children belong to you."

"I couldn't stay away from them any longer." Jeannie looked across at her brother. "And I felt so bad foisting them all on Blake. Once I knew Rod was okay, I got on the earliest flight I could."

"You should have called," Blake said. Ana looked at him, but he avoided her eyes. His cheeks were flushed, and he held his mouth tight.

Jeannie smiled at him, obviously not picking up on the tension between them. "I know how hectic it is with those five, and I didn't want to overexcite them either." She turned to Ana. "I didn't know you and Blake were still in touch?"

Blake interrupted before Ana could answer. "Ana arrived on my doorstep about two minutes before you did on Friday. She's been a wonderful help all weekend." He shot her a steely look. "She was just leaving."

Heat ran up Ana's neck and she returned Blake's unsmiling gaze. "It was my pleasure. We've discovered we are just the same people we were back in university. Isn't that so, Blake?" She bestowed a saccharine sweet smile on him and turned to Jeannie. "I was just about to say goodbye to Blake when you arrived. I have some things I really must do this afternoon."

She said a quick goodbye to Jeannie and the children and hurried to collect her overnight bag before Blake could follow and throw any more insults her way. She was so angry at his attitude, she needed to get away before she lost her temper and blew any chance of a rational conversation with him. As she closed the car door and put the key in the ignition, he ran down the steps and out to the car. He reached in and put his hand over hers on the steering wheel.

"Is he your boyfriend or did he just take advantage of your soft heart?"

Ana gritted her teeth, but she couldn't stop the angry words spilling out of her mouth. "How dare you make assumptions, Blake. As usual you are so wrong." She turned the key and the engine fired as she pressed the accelerator to the floor. "You haven't changed one bit, have you?"

"Nor have you, Ana. Still running away when things get tough."

A red mist settled in front of her eyes and she sat back with her arms folded across her chest. "Oh, but I have changed. Get in the car, Blake and I'll tell you why I'm here."

"I'm not interested. Tell your boyfriend he wasted his time sending you." Blake squatted down beside the open window and his head and shoulders filled the small space. "I think it's time you left, Ana." The afternoon sunlight gleamed off the bluish-black lights in his hair as he stared at her, a nervous tic jumping in his cheek.

So Mr Boss Man isn't as in control as he is trying to appear to be.

Ana forced a smile onto her face. She reached out and trailed her fingers down his cheek and paused on the pulse she could see beating in his cheek. "I'll make an appointment and come back when you are in a more approachable mood."

"I don't think there's any need for that." He caught her fingers in his and they stared at each other for a moment before she pulled her hand away.

"Oh, don't you worry, Blake. We'll be seeing each other again."

Blake stepped back as she put the car into gear and pulled out onto the road. Glancing in the rear-view mirror, she scowled to herself as the car reached the bottom of the hill. He was still standing on the side of the road looking her way. In the end things had ended up going exactly the way she'd expected.

***

Blake pushed the door open and stepped into the living room. Jeannie was sweeping up the crumbs by the side of the sofa where Billy had eaten his lunch.

"You don't have to do that. I'll get the cleaning service in tomorrow," he said.

"Really, Blake it's just a few crumbs. Once I pack up their gear and we're gone, you'll barely know they've been here."

"Are you going to take the laundry, too?"

"Be thankful I packed the disposable nappies, little brother. I use cloth ones at home." Jeannie laughed. She looked across at him curiously. "I didn't know you'd stayed in touch with Anastasia. Things seemed a bit tense between you."

"I didn't. She just turned up here. She was just telling me why when you arrived."

Blake flopped onto the couch and put his arm along the back of the seat behind the twins, drumming his fingers on the leather. The house was starting to look like his again now that Jeannie had packed up all the toys. A soon as they left, he was going to do some investigating into this restoration guy who had sent Ana.

Jeannie shot him a curious glance as she bustled past him with an armful of toys.

"You look upset. It wasn't that bad having the kids here, was it?"

"No." Blake jumped up and hugged his sister. "Just some business worries on my mind."

By the time Billy woke, the car was packed, and the children were lined up for a hug from *'Unca'* Blake.

"I'll come over and visit later in the week," Blake promised. "I've decided to take a drive to Maleny tomorrow to check out the store."

"Does Ana still live up there?"

"I guess she does," Blake said thoughtfully. "We were so busy looking after the kids we didn't get to catch up."

"It would be sweet if you could get to know her again." Jeannie stood beside the car as the children climbed into the back seat. "You know Ana had a crush on you back then."

"Maybe." Blake held him arms out for the baby so Jeannie could secure the children into their seats. "But mostly I was always the big bad landlord."

"You were grieving for Mum and Dad, Blake, and you always took your responsibilities so seriously." Jeannie gave him a quick hug before she opened the door. "You need to lighten up and start enjoying life."

The noisy farewell of the children stopped him from answering but his sister's soft words reduced his anger a little. He'd been very hard on Ana, but the thought of her being used by some incompetent handyman to come and plead on his behalf had stirred him up. It wasn't her fault that she wore her heart on her sleeve. She'd always been up front about the way she was.

Jeannie interrupted his musing as she lowered the car window. "I really owe you one, little brother. You have a good week."

Anticipation curled in Blake's stomach as he thought about the week ahead. He would track Ana down and get to the bottom of this. The anger burning in him had pushed away any thoughts about the store takeover which was most out of character for him.

"I intend to, sis."

Chapter Seven

On the way home Ana dropped into Thelma and Mitzi's farm to see if they still needed her help, but Georgie had visited earlier and had already moved their crates to their small shed. The two elderly ladies pressed her to stay for tea, but she'd declined. She had to find Sienna and Georgie. It was time to come clean and tell them the whole story.

"I suppose you have to mow the lawn and do your odd jobs." Thelma admonished her, wagging a finger in her face. "It's well past time you found a husband and sat home having babies."

Ana fought a giggle as a ludicrous picture of sitting in her cottage popping babies out came into her head. Then the smile faded as she remembered the feel and sweet smell of little Jake's downy head against her face.

Sure, she wanted a houseful of kids one day, but first she had to sort her work life out and make sure she could keep their business going somehow.

And besides, she needed a husband first before she could sit at home and pop babies out. She stifled another giggle. Blake popped into her mind and she tried to push their weekend together out of her mind.

Ana left the farm and drove through town to her next door neighbour's house at the bottom of the hill. Old Jerry loved looking after Mutt and walking him while she was at work, and he fed the cat and watched her house on the rare occasion she went away. In return, she mowed his lawn for him every second weekend and did odd jobs for him.

Ana whistled for Mutt to follow her and he bounded up the hill behind the car, pleased to see her home.

West of Maleny and well away from the Sunshine Coast and the dense suburban areas, Hill Cottage, her little house, was perched on a hill. Opening the gate, she called for the large clumsy dog to follow her into the garden. His head nudged her thigh as she put the key in the lock, and she reached down to scratch his head.

"Miss me, boy?" Soulful brown eyes looked up at her with adoration and she smiled at him, stepping back as he pushed past her into the kitchen. He headed for his basket by the window, totally at home inside the cottage. Blake could learn a lot from Mutt, she thought.

Huh, no pets in his house. He didn't know what he was missing out on. She squatted down beside the basket as the dog walked around three times before flopping down on the cushion. She scratched behind his ears. "Pets make a home, don't they Mutt?"

Ana stood and stretched, easing the tension from her body and trying to get Blake Buchanan out of her head. She averted her gaze from the shoe boxes on the table overflowing with papers and reached over to the kettle to brew some peppermint tea. Pouring some dog kibble into Mutt's bowl next to the door, she allowed herself a quick glance around the cottage. One day she would find the time to finish the various restoration projects she'd started here. Compared to Blake's house, her home looked like a—well, if she was completely honest—like a junk shop.

But this little cottage was hers and she loved every inch of it. As soon as she'd sorted out the problem with their jobs, finished the accounts, painted Thelma and Mitzi's kitchen like she'd promised weeks ago, she would start on the next room. She hated saying no to the old dears. It had only been a couple of months since she'd last painted it and they had decided they didn't like the colour. She had Sienna lined up for something special for them, but Ana had no idea when they were going to find the time to do the job.

There was always so much to do, and it was more important to fix the elderly folks' windows and leaky roofs than pretty up her cottage. Hers could wait, they needed to be warm and dry, and most of them couldn't afford a handyman. She frowned to herself as she thought of Blake and what he'd think of the set up.

Get out of my head, Blake. She shook her head impatiently. Two days in his company and he'd taken over her thoughts.

Her landline phone rang, and she scrambled through the paint tins and rolls of wallpaper beside the shoe boxes to pick up the old fashioned handset.

Sienna's voice greeted her. "Oh good, you're home. We're having a girl's night in—at your place. We're on the way. Is your house a mess?"

Ana looked around again and grinned. Sienna was just as bad as she was, and she wouldn't even notice the furniture covered in drop sheets. Georgie, however, would run around all night and try to clean up.

"The usual. If you're happy to perch at the kitchen table, you can help me with the accounts. Georgie can cook."

"No need. We've already ordered Indian from Raj. So there's no excuse for you. Tonight you come clean and tell us where you've been and all about this mystery man."

Ana sighed. "I was about to call you and invite you over anyhow. I think we need to make some contingency plans."

"We're on the way."

By the time Ana had a quick shower and pulled on some clean clothes, the lights of her work ute appeared at the end of her driveway. She knew it was her ute because one headlight pointed up to the trees and the other dropped down to the ground. She really had to get it fixed.

The smell of curry wafted in with Sienna and Georgie, and Ana smiled as Sienna pulled a bottle of wine from her bag.

"Spare beds are made up," she said.

"No. I'll only have one glass. I want my little red car back home safely in its own garage. That truck of yours is a heap, Ana." Sienna twisted the cork in the wine bottle until it gave a pop. Georgie put the bag of food on the counter, shoving one of the shoe boxes to make room.

"Okay, boss. Pull out the plates and spill all your news. Where have you been? I thought you'd run away with my car." Sienna put the ute keys on the dresser.

Georgie lifted her gaze from the containers of food. "You promised you'd tell us yesterday, but you've been as close-mouthed as Joe was when he was selling the store."

"Yeah, we don't want any more surprises here. You saw the head honcho on Friday when you borrowed the fancy clothes and my killer shoes. And then you disappear. That smacks of getting lucky to me." Sienna fixed a steely gaze on her.

Ana gave a sad little laugh. "I wish. Sorry girls, Blake is way out of my league. He was ten years ago, and he still is now."

"What do you mean out of your league?" Georgie shook a finger at her. "You have to stop putting yourself down because you dropped out of uni, Ana."

"Maybe." Ana folded up the corners of the kitchen tablecloth, drew them together like a swag, and lifted the cloth and its contents onto the floor. She pulled a clean cloth out of the bottom drawer in the old dresser and flicked it over the table. Sienna opened the cabinet and passed the plates and cutlery to Ana, while Georgie put out the food containers and poured their wine.

Ana picked up her glass and held it up. "To the future . . . whatever that may be."

Sienna groaned and the three girls clinked their glasses together before serving out the curry and rice. She placed her elbows on the table and pointed her fork at Ana while she chewed. "What happened?"

Ana knew she couldn't put them off any longer.

"Blake is as sexist and purely after profit as he was ten years ago. He's probably even worse. He just assumed I was there on behalf of some *guy*."

"So what did he say when you told him it was us—three women? What did he say to that?"

"That's the problem. I was so angry I left before I blew it completely." Ana loaded her plate with a second helping and held her glass out to Sienna for more wine. Ana took a sip closed her eyes as the image of Blake's smile stayed with her. "He can really be a nice guy."

"You're not making sense, Ana. He's either a nice guy and you can trust him, or he's not." Georgie sipped her wine and frowned.

"So just how close were you two in this share house?" Sienna's beautifully made up eyes were fixed on Ana's face. "There's something you aren't telling us."

Lifting her wine glass, Ana held it up and twirled it, and didn't meet Sienna's gaze. What had happened back then was between her and Blake and she wasn't going to share it. "We were just friends. I'll make an appointment to see him as soon as he hits town, okay?"

And I'll keep my temper this time. Waiting another couple of days wasn't going to make a difference. He'd either listen to her or they'd be out of a job.

Chapter Eight

Blake tucked his hands deep into his pockets and stood on the corner of Hastings Street waiting for the lights to change. He glanced over at the ocean, he could hear the hiss and roar of the waves from his house tonight. He'd bring Billy here one night; the little guy was fascinated by ocean. He was focused on his sea creatures.

Blake had managed to shake most of the fear that had stayed with him since Billy had teetered over that busy road, but now he shivered. One of the reasons he'd come back to Noosa was to be close to Jeannie and Rod and the kids. But when he had kids, there was no way he would stay in busy suburbia with its traffic and hidden dangers.

He blinked with surprise.

Where had that come from?

He had too much on his mind and his thoughts were skewing in a crazy direction. He needed to get them on track before he sat down with Mike.

Ana had been firmly fixed in his mind since she'd driven away this afternoon and now it was time to turn his thoughts to business. He had barely given the takeover a thought since he'd put his laptop away on Friday afternoon. For the life of him, he couldn't understand why she had come to plead the restoration guy's case. As soon as he arrived in Maleny, he was going to find her and get to the bottom of it.

And if he was honest, he owed her an apology. He'd been so shaken by what happened with Billy, he'd taken it out on her.

A cool breeze blew up the narrow street from the beach. When there was a lull in the traffic. Blake hurried down the hill and turned into the restaurant strip, looking for Fish Divine. He almost walked past—it was a tiny building on the corner, nothing like the restaurants in Melbourne where Mike usually held court. Pushing open the door, he looked around and spotted Mike and Helen sitting at a table tucked into the corner window overlooking the street.

"Blake." Mike's loud voice boomed out across the small space and some of the other diners smiled as he stood and enfolded Blake into a tight hug. "Great to see you, boy. What do you think of Noosa?"

Blake laughed and caught Helen's smile. "Hasn't changed much. Remember I grew up here, Mike?"

If it had nothing to do with making money, information didn't stay in Mike's head for very long. Before Blake could squeeze into the narrow space on the other side of the table, the bell on the door rang as it opened.

"Here's Jack!" Helen stood and waited for her son to cross the small restaurant before folding him into a tight embrace.

"Hey, mate." Blake reached over and shook Jack's hand when he'd extricated himself from his mother's arms. "What are you doing on the coast?"

"I'm moving to Noosa." Jack nodded at his father who sat tight-lipped, looking out the window, apparently engrossed in the traffic. "Dad."

Mike looked back at his son as Jack squeezed into the other side of the table next to Blake. "Son."

There was an uncomfortable silence for a few seconds until Blake turned to Jack. They'd met a couple of years ago and hit it off instantly over a few rounds of golf at the exclusive Royal Park Golf course in Melbourne where Mike was a member. Last Blake had heard, Jack had been commissioned to do a series of paintings for the club.

"So why the move to the coast?" he asked.

"I'm buying a gallery in Noosa. And I'll have peace and quiet to paint. Melbourne interferes with my creative process."

Mike gave a loud harrumph noise and picked up the menu. "Time to order, and then Blake and I have business to discuss."

After a few moments of casual conversation, Mike left to go to the rest room and Helen turned to Blake with an apologetic smile.

"Just ignore this pair. Mike is still cross that Jack doesn't love the business like he does. You know what he's like." Helen looked across at her son. "And Jack likes pushing his buttons."

"He'll get over it," Jack shrugged. "And if he doesn't, I don't really give a shit."

"Jack!" Helen glared at him and turned to Blake.

"Now before you get buried in business talk, tell me about your place here,' Jack asked. 'Are you going to drive to Maleny every day?'

"I'd like to stay in my house, but I suppose it will depend on the drive and"—he glanced across at Mike who was walking back to the table— "and the hours I'll have to put in to get the store up and running."

"Knowing Dad, he'll expect twenty-four seven." Jack glanced at his father who had stopped at the small bar on the other side of the restaurant.

"The takeover of the Maleny store was really a bonus for me. I'd planned on moving back home to Noosa anyway. It was time for a change," Blake said.

"Don't let Dad hear you say that," said Jack. "You're his golden boy."

"Hear what?" Mike sat back down and grinned. "Don't use the restroom, it's made for midgets." He patted his large girth with a huge hand. "And I'm no midget."

They all laughed and the atmosphere gradually lightened as they ordered and enjoyed their seafood meals. Jack and Blake caught up on the two years since they'd last met and even Mike appeared interested in some of his son's stories. After they'd finished their coffee, Mike summoned the waiter again.

"Who's going to join me in a port?"

Helen glanced across at her son. "Jack, would you walk me back to the hotel while these two talk business?"

As they said goodbye, Blake shook Jack's hand. "Want to come for a drive with me tomorrow? I'm heading down to Maleny to have a look around the area. We might throw the golf clubs in. What do you think?"

"Sure, give me a call in the morning."

Once they'd left, Mike turned to Blake and lifted his glass of port.

"To success in the latest Home and Hardware venture."

They clinked their glasses and Mike frowned. "So, how did it go with the guy who was coming to beg to save his department?"

"He didn't show. He sent someone else to plead his case, but we didn't have time to talk."

"Oh, well. He was going to get a big no, anyway, no matter who he sent. Stupid idea running tradesmen from a store. Just the cost of insurance alone would eat into any profits it made." Mike refilled their glasses. Blake knew where Mike's huge girth came from—he was a connoisseur of fine food and wine. Even though he was a member of the exclusive golf club, he'd never once seen him out on the course. "There's no place for softness in our business. If we listened to all the soft hearts, we would never make a dollar. And we can't have that, can we, son?

Blake cringed. He hated it when Mike called him 'son'. Even though he admired his boss for the successful corporation he'd built up, he thought Mike's priorities were a bit screwed. Seeing the way Mike treated his own son tonight had showed him how hard his boss could be.

"There's no place for any personal relationships in business. All those stores we've taken over, all those stores that wanted to be family businesses." Mike shook his head and took a gulp of his wine. "Bound to fail. There's no friendship in business. You remember that, son. As soon as friendship comes in the door, profit flies out the window."

Mike's loud voice drowned out the soft conversations in the small room and Blake flinched when he called him son again. A picture flashed through his head. If he devoted himself to Mike's philosophies, he could end up just like Mike.

Look what it had done for him. He was pretty much estranged from his own son and focused solely on chasing new business and bigger profits every year.

"The restoration guy was probably some old-timer, probably too old to drive himself into the city to see you. Joe, the owner, told me most of the staff is past retirement age." Mike's deep laugh boomed out and the restaurant went quiet as conversations paused while everyone looked at Mike. Blake looked down at his wine glass as discomfort crept through him.

"I have a mental picture of all the staff pushing themselves around the store on walkers. They can all be pensioned off and you can hire some fresh, young blood." Mike slammed his glass down onto the table and belched.

Blake folded his napkin and stood. He'd heard enough. "I'm going to the store tomorrow, just to get a feel for the place."

"Don't let them know who you are. Just wander in as a customer." Mike's hearty laugh boomed out. "Like one of those secret shoppers."

"Maybe. It's a good way to see how a place really works." Blake waited while Mike signed the bill. "Thanks for dinner. I'll call you after the handover on Friday."

Mike stood and eased his huge girth around the tables as he followed Blake to the door. "You'll have no trouble turning it around. Once we do the shop refit and turn it into a proper store, the folks down on the coast will come in droves. It's all about profit, profit, profit, boy."

Blake frowned at Mike's words. He had enjoyed the challenge of working with Mike's company and had supervised the takeover of several of the other stores but always from his office in Melbourne. This was the first time he'd actually been out on the frontline of a takeover and he wondered if Mike had taken the logistics of the small town atmosphere into account, particularly when there were local jobs being shed. It was the sort of thing he and Ana had argued about at uni.

"What do you mean by a proper store?"

Mike shook his head and frowned.

"Apparently Joe Hickey has owned it forever—like sixty years. He brags about how he's kept it looking like something from the last century. Nothing modern, not even checkouts at the front of the store." He shook his head and disbelief was written all over his face. "He's proud that they've never remodelled. They even have a slogan, if you can believe it in this day and age—a store slogan!"

"Which is?" Blake had never seen Mike so stirred up and uncertainty began to filter through him. It sounded like this takeover was going to involve a lot more changes than implementing policies and updating the storefront. His gut churned as he wondered what he was going to find down in this small community, and an uneasy feeling crept up his spine as he wondered if it was an old guy Ana was helping out. If he was honest with himself, it was jealousy that had pushed him into being so hard on her. Now it was beginning to sound like the Ana of old. Helping out the needy and not worrying about money.

"*Whatchamacallits, thingamajigs, and doohickies for every need.*" Mike choked on the words as he laughed, and Blake thumped him on the back.

"Interesting," Blake said. If he'd known all this about the store, he may have reconsidered the move and looked for another corporate position in Brisbane. He could have commuted from Noosa. As he always did, he'd looked at the figures and profit margins and he'd never had anything to do with human resources before. Maybe it was time he changed the way he thought, but he'd given his word to Mike and he'd see this deal through. The thought of seeing Ana again sweetened the deal considerably.

Chapter Nine

Joe had asked them to take inventory of the store so Magda could enter the stock into the computer. The renovation section area in the back was the only department waiting to be finalised.

Along with the accounts still sitting in the shoeboxes on her kitchen counter. Ana found it so hard to say no to anyone who needed help and it constantly put her behind. Balancing the accounts was the job she always put last because she knew the numbers never showed quite as much profit as they hoped to bring in. And definitely not as much as Blake would be expecting.

They'd ended up finishing the bottle of wine last night and when Sienna and Georgie had finally roared off in Sienna's little red sports car, Ana lit the candles on her bathroom windowsill and soaked in a deep bath. By the time she'd gotten out, she'd stumbled sleepily to bed.

Tonight. She'd do them tonight after the three of them helped out in the store.

"Well, looky here." Sienna drawled.

Ana lifted her head from the box of brass curtain hooks and frowned at Sienna. "What? Oh drat." She dropped the handful of hooks back into the box. "Now I've lost count." She looked up crossly at Sienna. "Look at what?"

"Three o'clock."

Ana put the box on the dusty concrete floor. "Are you going to stop talking in riddles? What's on at three o'clock?"

"Eye candy at three o'clock," Sienna dropped her voice to a husky murmur. "Georgie will be running for the wedding magazines when she sees this pair."

Ana rolled her eyes. "Are you going to help me count this stuff or do I have to do it all myself?"

"You are getting so boring. I think they might be movie stars or something. Oh, mama, huge and hunky. I heard there's a movie being made in the hinterland I wonder if they'd like to be shown around town. I'm just the girl for it."

"Sienna, you are supposed to be helping me, not planning your sex life." Ana sighed and pushed herself to her feet as Sienna reached for her phone.

God knows what she was texting. Sienna could be quite irreverent when the mood took her. A ripple of laughter came from Georgie in the next aisle and Ana craned over to read what Sienna had texted to her sister.

Sex on legs relief for those in need heading your way.

"You are so bad."

"Bad girls have more fun, don't you know that?"

Georgie appeared around the end of the aisle with a big grin on her face.

"Yes, I am in need. Where's the solution?"

She walked on her tiptoes in the direction her sister pointed and stood behind a pile of plastic wheelbarrows stacked almost to the ceiling.

"Oh. My. God." Georgie turned to Ana and beckoned her come over.

She wasn't going to get any peace until she looked at this eye candy of Sienna's and made the girls happy. Ana walked slowly to the end of the aisle and put her hand on Georgie's shoulder as she peered around the wheelbarrows.

"Oh, my God."

Georgie turned to her with a grin which died quickly when she looked at Ana.

Ana's world was about to come crashing down sooner than she'd planned unless she got out of there mighty quick. She recognised the jacket; she knew the hair and more than anything she recognised the butt she'd checked out thoroughly in the park yesterday.

What the hell is Blake doing here?

There was no way she was ready for this meeting with him today, not in front of everyone. The back door was at the end of the aisle where they were standing. If she could get to it before Blake—

and whoever he was with—turned around, she could go out and hide until he left.

As she spun around to make a quick exit, her shoulder knocked one of the wheelbarrows and it tipped slowly.

"Georgie, look out," she whispered urgently. But Georgie had turned to look at the two guys and didn't see the teetering pile tipping toward her. Ana shoved her out of the way just as the tower of wheelbarrows slid to the right and fell with a huge crash. As soon as she could see through the clouds of dust rising from the concrete floor, Ana checked that Georgie was okay and then she took off back down the aisle toward Sienna, who was standing next to the boxes of curtain accessories with her mouth wide open.

Gesturing madly to Sienna to open the back door, Ana didn't see the box in front of her and before she knew it, she sprawled headlong onto the floor. The hard concrete jolted against her ribs and took her breath away. She closed her eyes and buried her head in her arms, praying that no one would notice her spreadeagled on the floor while she tried to get her breath back.

The cold concrete pressed into her cheek and she slowly opened her eyes.

"Ana, are you okay?" Georgie crouched beside her and ran her hands up and down her back. "Ana, talk to me."

"I'm okay." She lifted her head and groaned as two pairs of jean-clad legs hurried down the aisle towards them.

***

As he and Jack approached the store, Blake wondered how much research Mike had done into the location. The village atmosphere of the small town seemed to be a real tourist attraction. It was certainly not the right place for a modern hardware store. Other stores surrounding it had been done up to retain the history of the place. Once they entered the dark and musty store, Blake had muttered and sworn under his breath at the mess. Piles of goods blocked fire exits, stock that looked to be decades old lay covered in dust on the shelves and the staff—God, Mike was right—Blake hadn't seen anyone under seventy yet.

"Why the hell did your father buy this place?" he whispered to Jack as they'd moved half a dozen large garden forks completely blocking one aisle. "He's got rocks in his head."

Jack grinned. "You're not telling me anything new there, mate."

"It needs demolishing." Blake ran his fingers through his hair in frustration. "How the hell—"

The crash of the wheelbarrows and the woman lying on the floor were all Blake's nightmares about this store coming to life. He and Jack took off at a run and were soon lifting the wheelbarrows to clear a space to the aisle.

A potential lawsuit already. Then he breathed a quick sigh of relief, they hadn't signed the paperwork yet.

Jack followed him and in the middle of the aisle, a woman was crouched down beside a prone figure face down on the ground with a silver blonde ponytail poking through a baseball cap. Blake hurried down past the piles of garden tools and crouched down beside her. He groaned. He must be hallucinating.

"Ana?" She rolled over to her back and looked up at him. Her jeans were filthy, and her dark jacket was covered in fine, grey concrete dust. A small bruise was darkening on her chin and he prayed she had no broken bones or concussion.

"Help me up, please."

"No, we have to make sure nothing's broken."

"I'm okay." She put her hands on the filthy floor and pushed herself up.

Blake looked around and spoke to the young woman crouched beside him. "Call an ambulance, please."

Before the woman could answer him, Ana interrupted crossly, "No, don't. I'm all right." Blake took her arm to steady her as she stood.

"Thank you. Now I'm in a hurry—I was just leaving." She pulled her jacket closed and stepped away.

"Wait, you can't just go. You have to give your details to the store so they can do a report." Blake held tightly to her arm. "You might have a concussion."

"I'm alright, Blake. Now I really have to go. I have more shopping to do."

The young woman beside him made a peculiar noise and he turned to her.

"Are you with Ana?"

"Er, yes. You could say that." The woman frowned at him. "I'm Georgie. And you're Blake?"

Blake nodded absently as he watched Ana hurry down the aisle toward the entrance of the store. "Tell her I'll call her."

Georgie waved to a woman standing at the other end of the aisle. "We'll pick you up later, Sienna . . . after we finish our *shopping*." She hurried out the door after Ana, while the woman she'd called Sienna sauntered up to them.

"Gentlemen, is there something I can help you with?"

Blake noticed the writing across the front of her T-shirt as she unfolded her arms. *'Whatchamacallits, thingamajigs, and doohickies for every need'*

"You work here?"

She nodded and stared at him. "Surely do. Now what can I help you gentlemen with?" Jack stood beside him not saying anything but paying close attention to their conversation.

Blake shook his head. "Ah, nothing. We were just leaving." Before he turned away, he cleared his throat. "You know Ana?"

"Yes, I do." The frown on the woman's face deepened and he could have sworn she was scowling at him.

God, were they all crazy in this town?

"So you know where she lives?" he asked.

"Yes, I do." She refolded her arms across her chest.

"Will you give me her address? So I can go check on her?"

"No, I won't. She's fine."

Blake shrugged and walked away as Jack followed.

If she wouldn't tell him, he might be quick enough to see Ana's red BMW parked outside and catch her before she left. He strode down the cluttered aisles as quickly as he could and stepped out into the spring sunshine. It was a pleasure to take in a deep breath of fresh air after the mustiness of the dark, cluttered store.

"Come on, Jack. I need a drink. I've got a lot of thinking to do."

There was no sign of Ana or her car, so they headed towards the hotel on the corner. While Jack found a table, Blake bought them a couple of beers from the bar and ordered a bowl of wedges.

He joined Jack at the table by the window, pulled out his phone, and sent a quick text to Ana's number asking her if she was okay.

"Who's Ana?" Jack asked curiously.

"An old friend from uni. I actually caught up with her over the weekend."

"Well, you must have made a great impression, mate. She couldn't wait to get away from you."

"Hmm." Blake stared into his beer and thought about the coincidence. Ana was connected to the store somehow and she'd let him believe she was on a social call until she'd come clean about being his appointment.

Read about me in the paper? He didn't believe a word of it. There was something smelly about the whole situation and he was going to get to the bottom of it.

"If you squeeze that glass much harder, it's going to pop. Waste of a good beer." Jack was looking at him curiously. "What's got you so upset? Not happy that the little cutie took off? I might get her phone number from you when I move down here."

Blake's head snapped up and he glared at Jack.

"Ah, so that's the way the land lies." Jack gave a quiet laugh. "Don't tell Dad you're interested in one of the staff."

"Staff?" Blake frowned. "What do you mean?"

Jack shrugged. "I might be wrong, but she had the same shirt on as the other girl who worked there. I noticed it before she pulled her jacket together."

***

Ana pulled Georgie along behind her as she crept around to the back entry of the store. "You go in first and check that they've gone. I don't want Blake to know that I work here, just yet."

"Why not? What on earth are you up to, Ana?" Georgie sighed. "And who's the hunky guy with your Blake?"

"I didn't want to talk to Blake yet. It really threw me when I saw him in the store." Ana replied

135

sheepishly. "And he is not *my* Blake . . . and I don't know the other guy."

Georgie grinned. "Could have fooled me. You're acting like a crazy teenager."

She waited outside until Georgie came back and called to her in a melodramatic whisper.

"Coast's clear."

Sienna was waiting inside the door and held her hands out to Ana. "Are you okay? That was a nasty fall you took." She reached up and touched her chin lightly. "Why the subterfuge?"

"I'm fine, just my pride was hurt. I was not going to have it out with him with an audience. And I'm angry."

"Because the wheelbarrows fell on you?" Sienna frowned at her. "I told Joe he had them stacked up too high when he bought so many last year."

"No, no." Ana put her hands on her hips. "I'm angry because that lowlife came sneaking around the store, checking it out. And did you notice? He didn't even go and see Joe. Joe obviously had no idea he was here, or who he was."

She stomped off toward the office. "I'm going to tell him."

Before she could get to the end of the aisle, Sienna caught up with her and grabbed her arm.

"And what's that going to achieve? You're overreacting." Sienna frowned at her.

"Don't go upsetting Joe and Magda. Let's go and grab some lunch and we'll work out what needs to be done."

Sienna glanced over at Georgie who was restacking the wheelbarrows into three piles instead of one high one. "Go grab our bags. I'll check if the street's clear."

As they walked through the store, Ana looked around her, trying to see the store through Blake's eyes. She'd worked here for ten years and was used to the dark and dusty interior. In fact, she even thought it added to its quaint charm. Blake would see it totally differently; he would see the clutter and chaos that she had always thought was quaint.

Georgie caught up to them as they stepped out into the street. The late morning sun was warm, and Ana shrugged off her jacket and brushed the remaining concrete dust off her store T-shirt. The street was busy as tourists meandered down the wide walkway between the old shops. It was a wonder the town wasn't under a heritage order. This town had been settled in the early twentieth century by Italian immigrants who had planted acres of vegetables to supply the Brisbane market, and it still had a distinctly European feel.

At the end of the street was a bar run by Sienna and Georgie's Uncle Renzo. Georgie disappeared into the kitchen to order their lunch and Sienna snagged them three stools at the counter.

"Drinks, girls?" Uncle Renzo called out.

"Just coffee, thanks. We're still at work." Sienna answered.

Ana propped her chin in one hand and gingerly probed her jaw with the other. She winced as her fingers encountered a tender spot.

Sienna took a quick breath beside her and Ana glanced up to see what was wrong. Reflected in the mirror behind the bar, she and Sienna were dressed in their dark work shirts with *whatchamacallits, thingamajigs, and doohickie for every need* emblazoned across their chests. Ana lifted her gaze higher and drew in a shaky breath before she turned slowly to face Blake who stood behind her with his arms folded across his broad chest.

"Hello, Ana."

"Hello, Blake."

"I take it you work at the hardware store?"

Beside them, Sienna's head turned from one to the other as they spoke.

"I do. And I take it you were creeping around spying before you take it over on Friday?" She kept her voice level.

Blake's eyes narrowed. "And I take it you're from the restoration department, and visited me to try and keep your job?"

If Ana had been royalty, she couldn't have inclined her head more gracefully then she did in response to his question. Ice-cold anger was building inside her and she fought to keep her temper under control.

"I was. However I saw a greater need and filled that."

'You haven't changed.' Blake gave a bitter laugh. "Always the do-gooder."

"And you are always the capitalist," she replied, holding his gaze without moving.

"Hey, you guys, time out." Sienna waved her hands between their faces, breaking their deadlocked gaze. Georgie came out from the kitchen and Blake stared at her T-shirt.

"All three of you work in restoration?"

"Yup." Sienna leaned in close to his face. "Hurt one, hurt all of us."

Ana frowned. "I can handle this, Sienna."

The guy who'd been with Blake in the store wandered over from the bar where he had been watching the exchange between Blake and Ana.

"Can I buy you a drink, ladies?"

"Are you going to introduce us to your *colleague,* Blake?" Ana asked.

"Not a colleague, just a friend out for an afternoon drive." The guy held his hand out to Ana. "Seeing as my pal here is so lacking in manners, I'm Jack."

She took his hand and introduced the two girls before sliding off the chair and pushing past Blake.

"Well, enough of the niceties. I'm going to call it a day. I'm feeling a bit . . . off." She glared at Blake as she turned to the twins. "I'll see you two tomorrow."

Ana turned on her heel and muttered 'nice to meet you' to Jack as she headed to the door.

Chapter Ten

Ana crunched through the gears and floored the accelerator of her ute—not that it made one scrap of difference. The old heap was ready for the wreckers and the engine groaned up the last hill to her cottage. Mutt was sitting at the back door waiting for her, as she stepped out and pushed open the gate to the cottage garden. She sat next to the big dog and put her arm around his neck. A sloppy, wet lick up the side of her cheek brought the first glimmer of her good humour back to her since she'd left the store.

"It's true what they say, boy. Pets lower the blood pressure. Would do Blake a load of good." She laughed as Mutt put his paw on her knee and tried to burrow his head under her arm. "You're certainly good for the soul." She ruffled his ears and stared out over the mountains. A huge bank of cloud was sitting above the horizon and a slight breeze was puffing wisps of cloud closer to the Glasshouse Mountains. The movement of the air was stirring the flowers in the garden and the sweet smell of orange blossom drifted in from the orchard on the hill across the fence.

Ana pushed herself to her feet, threw her bag on the old wooden bench outside the back door, and walked down to the small garden shed. Slipping on her gloves, she picked up the secateurs and headed into the orchard. Gardening was food for her soul and the combination of the view of the ocean and her pretty garden would bring her temper back to within normal range.

She even allowed herself a smile. She'd almost clocked Blake when he had called her a do-gooder. He hadn't changed one bit—he was still more interested in money and profits than people and that didn't bode well for their little hardware store. The compassionate, caring Blake she'd seen with the children was only what she'd wanted to see. He was as hard as nails. There was no hope for them.

Ana wandered around the orchard, clipping off dead branches and gathering a spray of blossoms to put in the kitchen. Holding the white flowers to her chest, she inhaled their sweet fragrance and stood on the cliff top as thoughts flitted in and out of her mind. The bright pink of the pig face plant at the top of the cliff years ago was a riot of colour and further brightened her mood.

Change was coming—as surely as the clouds would roll in over the hills this afternoon. There was no doubt about that. It was just a matter of making the right decision and adapting to the change. The soft purr of a vehicle reached her ears, and she knew it was Blake before she even looked. Happiness flitted through her briefly at the memories of their uni days. Their arguments may have been heated but inevitably one of them would seek the other out and apologise before the day was over.

With a deep sigh, she walked slowly across the orchard and stood at the gate watching as a sleek grey Mercedes drove up her rutted driveway. With the bouquet grasped in front of her, she waited while Blake parked the car.

He stepped out and walked across the lawn and looked past her to the mountains. "Nice view."

"Suits me fine," she replied, keeping her voice cold. "Who told you where to find me? Georgie?"

He nodded.

Ana sighed and shook her head. "Well then, now you're here, you'd better come in so we can have that chat."

She passed him the blossoms and smothered a smile as he stood there holding them while she pulled her gloves off. Taking them back, she turned and led him through the gate into the house garden. Mutt came up and sniffed around the back of the hand Blake offered him, before licking it and flopping back down in the shade.

"I guess that means one of you accepts me." His face was serious, and she found it hard to read his expression.

"It's nothing personal, Blake. We have business to discuss. We gave up the personal stuff ten years ago. A one night stand doesn't make us friends." Ana pushed open the back door. "We have nothing in common. And we never did."

She could feel his gaze on her as she walked into the kitchen. Crossing to the sink, she filled a large glass jug with water, put the orange blossoms in it, and carried it over to the table by the window.

"Sit down." She gestured to the only chair that wasn't covered with tools and rolls of wallpaper. "I'm renovating, so I won't apologise for the mess."

She stared at him, daring him to make a comment about the chaos surrounding them. Pressing fingertips to her forehead, she waited for the smart remark, but he surprised her with an apology instead.

"I'm sorry I was rude to you at lunchtime, Ana, especially in front of your friends."

Moving away, she bent down and cleared the other chair before replying. "I'm sorry, too. I was out of line."

Blake walked across and sat down. He leaned forward and dangled his hands between his knees, looking down at the floor. The sun broke through the clouds and shone into the room, illuminating the dust disturbed when Ana had cleared the chair. She watched him for a while without speaking, drinking in the sight of his broad shoulders, outlined by the snug T-shirt. A warmth she didn't want to feel, filled her chest and anger seeped into her voice as an attempt to disguise it. "Seeing as we are going to have a business meeting, we could probably do with some coffee? I know I could."

Blake went to stand, and she shook her head.

"No, stay there." Her mood softened marginally. "But thanks for offering."

While the coffee brewed, she reached up to the cupboard for two clean coffee mugs, but they were all in the dishwasher, which she hadn't run for a couple of days. She reached to the back of the cupboard and pulled out two fine china cups and saucers. It was a business meeting, so she would act like it was the usual way she entertained her clients. Ana looked across at Blake, the cups rattling as her hands shook. He was watching her with an intense expression on his face. His lips were straight and frown lines creased his forehead. Looking away, she filled the tray and added some of the ANZAC bikkies Thelma had sent home with her on Sunday.

Placing the tray on the floor between the two chairs, she sat and waited for him to break the silence. When Blake didn't speak, she bit her lip and reached down to the tray, ignoring the thudding of her heart. The silence continued as she passed him a black coffee and placed a cookie on the saucer.

Finally she couldn't stand it any longer and took a sip of her coffee before blurting out, "So where do we start?"

Blake put his cup down and folded his arms. "You made the appointment with me last week, so I'll listen to what you have to say. I'll be fair and give you the same consideration you would have had"—his voice was cold— "in your business suit and high heels."

Ana took a deep breath and relaxed into the soft sofa, reassured by his apparent willingness to hear her out but her heart was still pounding heavily.

"Okay." She met his steady gaze. "This town is very special. Down on the coast is the commercial centre where businesses like Home and Hardware should go. Maleny is for people who have lived here all their lives, and for those who retire here for a slower—more old-fashioned, I suppose you could say—lifestyle. It has created a unique place that tourists love, and flock to."

She looked down and that ever present shiver when he was around trickled down her back. She rubbed her arms to dispel the goose bumps.

"The renovation department, specifically Georgie, Sienna and I, provide a service. It's so important to keep the old homes true to their original state, and we've combined our skills to restore them." She jumped out of the chair as a thought struck her. "Finish your coffee. We're going for a drive so I can show you some of the houses we've done."

Blake shook his head and her spirits plummeted.

"I'm sure the work you do is great. But I need to see how much money it makes."

Ana couldn't stop herself from glancing at the shoe boxes full of invoices. The goose bumps disappeared as heat crept up her neck. She dropped her head and her hair fell over her face as she attempted to hide the tell-tale red flush she knew would be staining her fair skin. All was quiet for a moment and she fought to regain her composure. Lifting her head, she dug deep for the anger she'd felt the other day when he'd made assumptions about her.

"You could give us the courtesy of looking at our work. You obviously don't think women are capable of doing it. Then if—"

"Whoa. Stop right there." Blake came over and crouched in front of her. "Where did you get that idea from?"

Ana pushed to her feet and crossed to the window. When he was near her, she couldn't think straight and her whole future—and that of her friends—hung in the balance.

"Ana, look at me." She lifted her gaze to meet his and to her distress a single tear spilled over on to her cheek. Blake followed her and he lifted one hand and wiped it away with the pad of his thumb. "What makes you think I am such a sexist? Surely not that silly argument we had back in college?"

"No . . . well, yes. I suppose that was part of it. And then you made that comment about a guy sending me on Friday to plead his case. You automatically assumed it would have been a man."

Blake's voice was patient. "No, Ana. My secretary told me *a guy* was coming for the appointment. There was obviously a mix-up because I made no such assumption."

"Coming to see you was going to be our—or rather my —final attempt to save our jobs. Joe had already told the staff which departments would be going and who would probably be out of work. I thought I'd appeal to you—and maybe your commitment to the community. I knew how important your family home was to you and I thought you might understand."

"Business doesn't run on kindness . . . or friendships." Blake smiled and ran his fingers down the side of her face. "Ana, you always were a softie. Going into a competitive industry where it's all about pleasing shareholders never would have suited you."

"But Blake, why does it have to be like that? We've managed here this way for a long time." She reached for his hand. "You've seen the store now, and you've seen our little town. You have to see that it isn't the type of place that a big shiny store will fit in."

"If you had asked me the same question on Friday at my place, I wouldn't have understood. Now I've been to Maleny and seen the store, I get more of a sense of where you are coming from."

He looked at her intently and she swallowed, desperately trying to keep her gaze from his lips. She tried to let go of his hands, but he gripped hers tightly.

"Look, I'm probably going to regret this, and I can't promise anything, but I'd like to sit down with you and have a look at the numbers from your department. I don't remember seeing them in the spreadsheets Mike sent me."

She shook her head. "No," she said slowly." Magda is just waiting for me to get last . . . er . . . the last couple of month's figures to her."

"Are they on your computer? We could have a quick look at them now." He patted his shirt pocket and pulled out a flash drive. "I can take them with me and add them in with the others."

Ana couldn't help the bubble of laughter coming up from her chest and past her lips. Blake tipped his head to the side.

"What? Is it so funny I carry a flash drive around?"

"No." She pointed to the table. "I don't think you can transfer shoe boxes to a flash drive."

Blake looked to where she was pointing at the three overflowing containers. He turned back to her and smiled, the laughter lines crinkling around his blue eyes.

"Oh, Ana, you haven't changed a bit, have you?"

Ana caught her breath, the feelings she had been trying to push away since she'd first seen him last Friday rolled over her in waves, and she closed her eyes to block his face from her view. She tried to summon up a semblance of control as her nerve endings went into a tailspin as he stood close to her. There was silence for a moment and then gentle fingers gripped her chin again. She opened her eyes slowly.

"It's going to be okay, Ana."

Ana heard what he was saying but the words didn't really sink in. The expression on his face told her he wasn't really thinking business either. Silence stretched between them and she wondered if the same tingles were running up and down his arms as he held her gaze in his.

Don't get excited.

She wasn't going to get her hopes up because dreams didn't come true like that. He was just being kind.

"Right, then. Let's talk business," she said briskly smoothing her hands down the front of her jeans. "That's really the only thing we're here for, isn't it?" She crossed the room and picked up the first box.

***

The fact that Ana reminded him of their business relationship brought Blake solidly back to earth. Years of making high stake deals in boardrooms had taught him how to keep his expression bland. But when Ana stood in front of him grasping a blasted shoe box against the 'whatchamacallits' and 'doohickies' T-shirt, the sweet smile on her face sent all his resolve crumbling.

"Come outside with me. The table on the porch is clear."

While he waited on the porch, Ana made more coffee for them. By the look of things they would be here a while. It was only fair to listen to her. She'd put her life aside for him over the weekend and helped him with Jeannie's kids, so it was one way he could repay her a little bit. And besides, he loved being with her. Once she'd left, his house had seemed sterile and empty. Her enthusiasm for her work and the local community was infectious and he was prepared to listen to what she had to say.

No promises, but he'd listen.

He knew Mike would be immovable on changing the store structure. Every Home and Hardware store across the country was identical. The stock, the layout, the staff structure, and their uniforms—he'd argued a few times with Mike about the need to do a demographic study, but in his usual bull-headed form, the man wouldn't listen.

"Shit." Thinking about Mike reminded Blake of Jack waiting for him in town. He glanced down at his watch. It was just after two o'clock. Pulling out his phone, he scrolled through to Jack's number and pressed call.

"Hey, Blake."

"Sorry, Jack. I got caught up with some business. Do you mind if we skip that round of golf?"

"No problem. Georgie here—" Blake heard a feminine chuckle in the background— "has offered to show me around. I was just about to call and see how much longer you'd be."

"Great. I'll call you in a couple of hours when we finish."

"Sounds like a plan. See you later, mate."

The smell of freshly brewed coffee wafted out to Blake as he put the phone back into his pocket. He drew a deep breath and settled back into the comfortable chair. He grinned to himself—the porch was neat and tidy in contrast to the inside of the cottage. A deep planter running along the balcony was filled with a profusion of sweet-smelling herbs. Wind chimes hung on each side of the steps and as the afternoon breeze puffed in, the gentle tinkle of chimes overlaid the sound of the birds trilling from the bush.

The door pushed open and he jumped up to take the tray from Ana.

"I'll just get the boxes." She grinned at him and disappeared inside, reappearing with her arms laded with the three boxes.

"How long have you lived here, Ana?" Blake gestured around to the cottage.

"Do you mean in the cottage? I bought it about nine years ago after my mum—with a small inheritance, but it was in such a state of disrepair I didn't move in for a few months. Sienna and Georgie helped me do the kitchen and bathroom, so it was liveable."

"So you've been friends for a while?"

"Since the first day of school when we were five-years-old."

"I owe you a couple of apologies, you know." He looked out over the ocean searching for the right words.

"When my parents died in the accident, Jeannie and I were left in that huge old house in Toowong." He shook his head and reached for his coffee. "I knew Jeannie was going off to Sydney uni and I was terrified of being alone. So I filled the house with you guys and watched you all have a great time."

"You never really did join in with us," Ana said quietly. "I always felt we weren't good enough for you."

Blake stared down at his feet and scrubbed a hand through his hair. "I just didn't know how to connect with you all. So I guess I overplayed the landlord role a bit and, in the process, I really screwed things up."

He lifted his head and turned to face Ana. "I'm sorry about that last night. I always wondered if you left so suddenly because we slept together."

"Oh no, don't ever think that. I was upset and I didn't even think to leave you a note or anything."

"So why did you go?"

"I came back here to Maleny. I got a call. My mum was ill—dying. I left without thinking about anything else."

Blake wasn't aware he'd been holding his breath and now he let it out a light exhale. "For ten years, I thought you left uni because of me." He put his hand on her arm as distress filled her face.

"No, Blake. You couldn't be more wrong. That night was special for me and it stayed with me through some pretty tough times. I was young and Mum was all I had. I guess I didn't know how to handle my grief. And after she passed, the twins and I started up the business and it grew from there."

She leaned across and picked up a business card that was in the box with the receipts and invoices. "I'll never have the academic credentials you do, and I don't lead a glamorous corporate life, but we work hard, and we do okay." She passed him the business card and smiled at him. Her face came alight as she looked up at him and it was like a punch to his stomach. For a moment, he just looked at her, the light in her face as she told him about the business.

"We had so much work when our reputation began to build, Joe offered us the chance to run our own department out of the store. Georgie had worked there since she'd left school and Joe did the billing and the accounting, while Sienna pulled in the jobs. And we all did the restoration work."

Blake shook his head slightly. "I don't understand. If they do the business side, why do you have all this?" He gestured to the boxes.

Ana darted a sideways glance at him as she turned the pages. "The accounts that go through the store are the ones where we make the money. These other accounts are for the jobs that the store . . . er . . . subsidises. But is shows you how many jobs we have. Between the two types of jobs, and um . . . and the great profit the store makes on the other ones, these kind of—."

"Kind of what?"

Ana jutted out her chin. "Look, Blake. It's the sort of thing that happens in small towns where members of the community look out for each other."

"I'm not arguing. I just don't understand what you're saying." A prickle of unease trickled down his neck. He had a feeling he wasn't going to like her explanation.

"Okay, it's like this. We have two types of clients. There are the long-term locals who need work done to maintain their homes, and there are the outsiders who buy up the old houses to flip them. You know, they get us to renovate them and they make a profit."

"So you charge them differently?"

"One side of the business funds the other. The people who hire us to restore their houses so that they can flip them are happy. They make up for the money we spend on the old folks' maintenance jobs. Joe supplies the materials from the store, and we charge them at cost."

He scratched at his head. "So where's the profit come from?"

"Well," she said slowly. "There isn't a lot."

"And Joe was happy with this setup?"

Ana folded her arms. "Yes, he was. And he is."

"And what do you get out of it?"

Ana pursed her lips obviously trying to keep her response polite. He recognised the signs of her temper building from the old days.

"Apart from the satisfaction of helping people. I get a wage." She pushed herself to her feet and waved a hand over the boxes. "I'm not doing a good job of explaining here." She went back inside and came out with her car keys. "Come with me."

Blake followed her as she strode across to the old work ute beside his Mercedes and he thoughtfully climbed into the passenger seat.

Ana didn't speak as she backed down the steep driveway. Blake bounced in the seat as the wheels hit a rut and his head hit the roof of the car. He reached for his seat belt as they turned out onto the main road.

"Where are we going?"

"You'll see."

Chapter Eleven

Ana's heart was pounding, and heat was flushing through her body. She'd really messed that up. It had been ten years since she'd written all those great essays on welfare economics, and all the terminology could still roll off her tongue. But here she was talking to a corporate executive who had always bettered her in any argument.

Her hands gripped the steering wheel and she stared ahead at the road as it wound north towards the township, and then turned down to the coast. Blake didn't speak as she guided the car around the sweeping bends of the highway, and she focused on her breathing. Showing him the Bennett place was going to demonstrate how good their work was, but deep in her heart she worried it wasn't going to make the slightest bit of difference to his decision.

As they rounded the last curve, the house appeared in front of them, situated majestically at the top of a sweeping lawn with the real estate agent's for sale sign perched in the middle.

"Hmm," said Blake. "That's an exclusive agency. They're one of the best in the Noosa area."

"This is an exclusive house." Ana pulled up beside the fountain in the middle of the circular driveway and reached into the glove compartment for the house keys.

She put the key into the lock of the main entry conscious of him standing so close behind her, she could almost feel the warmth of his body. Smiling to herself, she turned her attention to his reaction to the house. He was about to get his socks blown off.

But when she turned to him, Blake wasn't looking at the house. His gaze was fixed on her and her heartbeat kicked up. Reaching out, he brushed a stray lock of hair back from her face. More heat surged through her. At this rate she'd look like she had a bad case of sunburn.

No matter how much she tried to convince herself they were too different, his touch sent her nerves jangling.

"So why are we here?"

"You'll see."

##

The Bennetts had employed a landscaping firm and staged the house with rented furniture. The only room without furniture was the ballroom where she and the girls had just recently completed the decorative plasterwork.

"This is why I couldn't help you out on Saturday. We had to finish up here." With one hand casually anchored on her hip, she led him through to the large room leading out to the balcony and swallowed a satisfied smile when he looked around.

Ana straightened her shoulders as she looked around with satisfaction. "Did a good job, didn't we?"

"What exactly did you do?"

"Everything." She spread her hands wide. "Plasterwork, painting, tiling, cupboards, varnishing—" Her voice trailed off as Blake walked into the kitchen and she followed him.

"The only thing we don't do is the plumbing and the electrics, but Joe's two nephews take care of that."

Blake walked over to the bench top and ran his hand along the gleaming granite before turning to her. "You, Sienna, and Georgie did *all* of this?"

"Yep."

"This is amazing. It's as good as anything I've ever seen." Slowly shaking his head, Blake turned back to her.

"Why wouldn't it be?" Ana laughed at the disbelief on his face. "Why do you look so surprised? And be careful of any sexist comment you might be thinking of making."

She studied him, standing in the room where she had worked her butt off for the past three months. A lurch in her belly hit her like a sucker punch. No matter what he thought of her, no matter what he said, she wanted him as much as she ever had. Despite their differences, his presence surrounded her and filled her senses. All the old feelings came rushing back and she tried to ignore the feelings flooding through her, but then Blake looked over and smiled at her.

"I can't believe you do this for a salary. Joe must be making a killing on this. He's obviously more astute than we gave him credit for."

Her happiness fizzled as if he had thrown a bucket of cold water over her. Just when she'd thought he was seeing the worth and beauty of their work, he had to bring it back to profit and balance sheets. He would never understand why they did it.

Always Mr. Cold and Calculating putting the dollar first.

Nothing had changed, she'd been kidding herself. He was still the same hard-nosed businessman chasing a dollar. He would never understand her.

For the life of her, Ana couldn't understand this damn attraction to him. It had to be just lust, because she didn't like one little thing about his attitude. She deliberately blocked out his kindness to his niece and nephews and his explanation about his loneliness when his parents died. It was all about money for him and it always had been. She couldn't believe she thought she was falling for him.

"No," she said coldly. "Joe gives back to the community."

"How?"

Turning on her heel, Ana strode to the door and flung it open. "Come on, I have something else to show you. It might not be as upscale as you're used to, but the work that goes into it is worth ten times more to me than something like this."

She'd shown him what she did and told him how Joe worked. Showing him Thelma and Mitzi's house might kill any chance of him taking her seriously, but she was going to be honest about what drove her to do the work she did.

And then the ball would be firmly in his business court.

***

Blake was sure Ana had an ulterior motive for showing him this job. The two elderly ladies fussed over him as he held a fragile teacup between his fingers and balanced a plate of cake in his other hand. Ana sat back with a smug smile.

"And we must show you the chicken coop too." The smaller of the two ladies reached over and held his arm—he thought it was Mitzi— and he couldn't move for fear of dropping his plate.

"Ana built it for us last winter. She is very clever, you know." The old dear dropped her voice to a whisper and he nodded, glancing across at Ana as a stifled chuckle came from her direction.

"Did we tell you she fixed our fence too?" the other woman added.

"And our roof was leaking, and she came out in the middle of the night, climbed up on the old wooden ladder to fix it while it was still storming." Blake's head turned from one to the other as they finished each other's sentences.

"And there was the time—"

"Mr. Buchanan has seen plenty of the house," Ana interrupted. "As soon as he finishes his tea, we'll have to go. He's very important." Blake narrowed his eyes as Ana smiled at him sweetly. "He's the new owner of Joe's store, you know."

The two old dears squealed with delight and sat on either side of him on the floral sofa.

"How wonderful! So you are going to be a part of our town." The one called Thelma patted his hand.

"You can come to the weekend markets. Do you do any woodwork or make things?" You could set up a stall." Mitzi hung on to his other arm. "And you will have to come to dinner with us."

Blake glanced across at Ana as she stifled a laugh.

"Thank you, I'll keep you to that." He smiled as Ana looked obviously surprised at his easy acceptance of the elderly women. "And I'm not the owner, just the manager and I'll be living in Noosa."

"Oh, no." Thelma grabbed his hand and shook her head. "Living there is too lonely. A nice young man like you needs to be part of a wonderful community like ours." She shot a smile at Ana. "If you are working here you will need to live close by. And you'll need to mix with other young people."

"And if you live close by you can come to dinner with us more often." Mitzi squeezed his hand. "Isn't that so, Ana? You tell him what wonderful cooks we are."

Ana caught his eye and grinned at him as she nodded. He had a feeling he was the centre of a matchmaking plot being hatched by the two women. But despite the teasing, he was surprised to find he was enjoying himself. "I would be delighted to come for dinner and try your home cooking. I don't see a lot of that. My sister has five children and when I eat at her house, we generally eat the same meal as the children." Blake couldn't remember the last time he'd spoken to anyone about his family. In fact, he doubted if any of his work colleagues even knew he had family back in Noosa. "I usually eat out at restaurants."

"That's dreadful! We'll have to take you under our wing." Thelma said.

"Like we did with Ana." Mitzi said looking across at Ana with a smile. "She eats with us often, don't you sweetie? After her poor mum passed on, we all made sure she looked after herself." Mitzi pulled a lace hanky from her pocket and wiped her eyes. "And now she's like a granddaughter to us."

"Not only us, she takes care of the whole community." Thelma stared at him. "I hope things won't change. It would be dreadful if Ana couldn't help us out." Discomfort filled Blake at the thought of the changes that were about to happen. He'd had no idea what Ana had meant when she'd talked about the jobs she did for the elderly folk, and he knew his answer wasn't what they wanted to hear. "Don't worry, Home and Hardware won't let you down."

Thelma reached for her walking stick and pushed herself to her feet. "Mitzi, give Mr. Buchanan another slice of cake." She turned to Ana. "Come into the kitchen, dear. We've chosen the new colours for the walls."

Blake glanced at Ana as Mitzi refilled his teacup and passed him another slice of cake. He knew Ana was enjoying herself. They left him sitting in the parlour—the room filled with old-fashioned furniture and knickknacks couldn't be called anything else—while the two women dragged Ana into the kitchen. Leaning back on the sofa, Blake closed his eyes trying to come to terms with everything he'd seen today.

He'd known Ana was kind—and generous. She'd put her own responsibilities on hold for a couple of days to help him out with the kids, but he hadn't realised this was how she lived her life. All of the philosophies she'd espoused at college were here in front of him, in flesh and blood, in real life, and Blake didn't know what to make of it.

She was important to these two women and by the sound of things, there were many more old folk who relied on her. This town seemed to be all about building relationships and giving back. And Ana was at the centre of it. It was alien to anything he'd ever experienced before. Jeannie had never called for his help before last weekend and really if he thought about it, he wasn't needed by anyone. An emptiness sat uncomfortably in his stomach and it had nothing to do with the food he'd eaten.

"Ssh, he's having a little nap." Blake's eyes flew open as the three of them came in laughing from the kitchen and he caught Ana's gaze fixed on him. Desire hit him fair and square as he caught a fleeting glimpse of hunger in her eyes.

He stood and turned to the two elderly women. "Thank you for showing me your cottage. Your home. It's delightful."

Blake followed Ana to the car as they waved them off. He was looking forward to getting home and thinking this through. The feeling that Mike was making a huge mistake was growing and he wasn't sure he wanted to be a part of it anymore.

***

The sight of Ana striding along the tiled floor toward the front door of that magnificent house stayed with Blake all week. Her cute little behind outlined by her snugly fitting jeans came into his head at the strangest times. And the feel of her lips beneath his. He shook his head to clear his thoughts—he had to focus on the Zoom meeting.

Mike was talking about profit margins and standardised stores, and all he could think about was how well Ana filled out her jeans.

"Blake? What do you think about that?" Mike's voice interrupted his musing,

"Sorry." Blake turned his attention back to his boss whose ruddy face filled his screen. "About what?"

"What's wrong with you? Don't tell me I've made a mistake sending you out there."

Blake balled his hands into fists at his side, biting down on the angry response that sprung to his lips.

"No, Mike. You didn't send me. I chose to move back here. Remember?"

Blake could see Mike's eyes narrow on his screen.

"You been spending time with Jack?"

"No. He's gone back to Melbourne. Why?"

"Thought it might explain why you weren't focused. Thought you might have been out partying."

Although he was loyal to the company, his boss's attitude was starting to piss him off big time.

Blake injected coldness into his voice and his words came out like steel pellets as anger burned through his chest. "I have been doing some research into this takeover and I think we might be making a mistake up here."

"Why?"

"Mike, have you even been to Maleny?"

"No need, the team sussed it all out. It's a prime site for future growth. I know it's not going to be a big store for a while, but Sunshine Coast is growing. In a few years, Maleny will be a suburb like any other and we'll already be established there, waiting for all the new homeowners to come and spend their money."

And what a shame that would be.

Blake swallowed. He couldn't believe the direction his thoughts were taking. Ever since Ana had shown him around the small community and he'd met Thelma and Mitzi, he'd become more uncomfortable about the takeover of the store.

"Blake, don't you worry about it. The figures have been run hundreds of times. There's enough business already to make the wait worthwhile. Once the area develops, it will take off big time. You just have to go in there tomorrow and get going. It won't be pretty, but that's the way we make money."

Blake lifted his head and stared at the screen. Mike's jowls were sagging, and his neck was pinched where the sides of his shirt struggled to meet beneath his chin. The veins on his cheeks were broken and contributed to the ruddiness of his complexion.

"There's just one more thing I want to run by you before we sign off." Blake kept his voice firm. "Have you thought any more about the restoration department? I've had a good look around the area and it's a huge business down here. *Spark and Burns Realty* has the market sewn up and the hardware store does most of the work on the restorations."

"No." Mike shook his head emphatically. "A standard store set up, remember? You go and sort out the human resources and the refit team will arrive in a couple of weeks."

A couple of weeks. And then a couple of dozen people would be out of a job, and Ana would be taken away from the work she loved.

Piece of cake.

##

The following morning, Blake dressed in his business suit and exited the hotel to his car. It had rained overnight, and the heavy grey sky matched his mood. Rolling down his window, he let the cool air blow in and listened to the swishing of the tires on the road, trying to concentrate as he drove from Noosa to Maleny. Joe had organised for him to talk to the whole staff before the store opened and then he had back-to-back appointments with individual staff members.

And he wasn't looking forward to any of it.

His stomach was in knots as he focused on the road ahead of him. Every time he thought about how to tell the staff about the upcoming changes, all he could picture was Ana's face when he had to tell her the restoration department was gone.

The street was jam-packed with cars when he pulled up outside the small hardware store. Stepping from the car, he avoided the puddles in the gutter and even that made him think of Ana and the wet shoes she'd carried into his place only a week ago. He schooled his face into a pleasant expression as an elderly man in a suit stepped from the store with his hand outstretched.

"Blake Buchanan?"

He took the proffered hand and shook it, appreciating the strong grip that grasped his hand in welcome. "Joe Hickey? Great to finally meet you in person."

And immediately his professional confidence came back, and he breathed a sigh of relief. It was time he got over this mooning around and focus on the job in hand.

Joe chatted to him as they made their way up the stairs to the office overlooking the store. The walls only went halfway to the ceiling and the noise of the store as the staff prepared to open for the day drifted up to them. A small, motorised trolley purred along one aisle and another elderly man swept with a straw broom, stirring up clouds of dust.

"We're very lucky here." Joe looked at him from beneath beetling brows. "When I told the staff about the meeting, they all came in early so the store could still open on time."

"Great." Blake rubbed his hands together briskly and peered down into the store. It was cool up here in this open-walled office and there appeared to be no heating in the old building. A quick glance down to the store below showed no sign of Ana yet.

"Here's the list of your appointments for the day."

Joe handed Blake a handwritten list of names and chuckled. "I hope you can read my wife's writing. She doesn't like to use a computer much— says they're too impersonal."

Blake ran down the list twice, but he didn't see Ana or Sienna on it.

"Is this complete?

"Yes," replied Joe. "Two of our girls resigned yesterday so you don't need to meet with them."

Chapter Twelve

The damp seeped through her jeans as Ana kneeled on the wet earth. She'd left her gloves in the shed and had intended to use the garden fork to turn over the soil in her vegetable garden. But the weeds had beckoned and now she sat back on her heels with wet knees and black soil covering her hands. Breathing in the smell of rain, she tipped her head back and let the light mist caress her face. Despite the weather, it was restful being outside catching up on her chores. The garden had been well and truly neglected since they'd started work on the Bennett house and the weeds had overtaken the vegetable patch. She grinned to herself. It was usually only the inside of her cottage that was chaotic.

And with the way things had turned out, her garden was going to be even more neglected from now on. If Home and Hardware wouldn't keep them on, then she and Sienna would just do the work themselves. It might be a little slower as they waited for materials instead of using the store's inventory, but they would still have jobs they loved.

She hummed to herself as she worked until the sound of a car coming up the drive interrupted her thoughts.

She wiped her hands on her jeans and wandered over to wait by the side of the driveway as Blake parked next to her ute.

At least I won't have to wait for Georgie to report in now.

Ana lifted her hands to give her hair a quick finger comb and remembered just in time that she had dirt all over them. Pausing with her hands in mid-air, she wondered what it was about Blake that always put her in such turmoil. It wasn't so hard to admit that just being around him excited her.

It always had been.

He stepped out of the car and tucked the keys into his suit pocket. Her nerves were jangling by the time he reached her.

"Hello, Ana."

"Hello, Blake." She stood and drank in the sight of him in his suit, trying to keep her expression solemn. "This is a surprise. I thought you'd be busy at the store?"

"I'm on my way back to Noosa and I just wanted to check on you." He frowned as he looked down at her. "Why did you resign so suddenly?"

Ignoring his question, she turned her back to him and headed inside. "Come in." He followed her and as she washed her hands, she watched as he lifted her cat from the sofa in the living room and sat down. Instead of putting the cat on the rug, he lifted Sooky into his lap and patted her.

The traitor lifted her head back between his hands and purred.

"You'll get cat hair on your suit."

He shrugged. "I've been thinking about getting a pet. Can't decide between a cat or a dog." He shot her a grin, but she didn't take the bait.

"That will be good for you."

"Yes, it probably will. Look, come over here and talk to me." Blake held her gaze until she shrugged her shoulders and sat at the far end of the sofa.

"Why did you resign?"

"Did anything change? Did management have a sudden change of direction?" Ana lifted her chin and waited for his reply.

"No."

"Then I did the right thing. No point staying where I'm not wanted."

Blake cleared his throat and she smiled. She was enjoying seeing him squirm.

"You have to understand, Ana. I did try."

"Oh, I'm sure you did, Blake. Once you'd seen the potential of our work, I'm sure the dollar signs went *ka-ching*."

"I really do admire your work."

"What? The moneymaking potential of what we do?" She held his gaze and held her resolve firm as he ran his fingers through his hair. She was starting to recognise his gestures and what they meant. "Don't you worry about us. We've taken our future in our own hands. Sienna and I are opening our own little business and we are going to be just fine."

"What do you mean?"

"Watching how you operate and listening to your endless talk of profit made me realise I wouldn't work for you even if you wanted us to stay. You have no care or respect for the community—for our people—and that's a given for us."

Blake slid across the sofa in one swift movement and grabbed her hands. "You're wrong about me, Ana. You have to understand I work for a large corporation and as such I have to remain loyal to the business direction, even if I may not agree with it."

"As such"—Ana mimicked his phrase— "you are selling your soul for something you don't believe in." She looked up and was encouraged by the uncertainty in his expression. "Why do you stay there, Blake? If you don't agree with what's happening?"

His eyes held hers and he frowned. "Up until the Maleny store, I've always worked in front of a computer. I've never had anything to do with the community, or the people in the store. It's never been real."

Ana pulled her hands away from his clasp, ignoring the need to stay holding onto him. She stood and moved across to the window. "Sounds like you've got some thinking to do then. Everything is real, we are real." She placed her hands on her heart. "The people you've met. Joe, Mitzi, Thelma and there are many more in this wonderful town—they're all real people with needs and feelings."

"Tell me about what you're going to do." He stood and put Sooky down carefully on the chair, but she shook her head.

"No way. You're the competition now." She smiled sweetly at him. "I'd hate to put you in a difficult position."

"Oh, for goodness sake, Ana. I'm here as your friend."

"Blake, we were never friends. You barely tolerated me at college. We slept together once, you used me when you needed help last weekend, and you were about to take my job away from me today. If that's what you call being friends, I'd hate to be your enemy."

"If that's how you feel, there's no point in me hanging around. I was going to see if you wanted to come back to town with me and have dinner."

She laughed bitterly. "What? You were going to fire me and then take me out to dinner? Now that does remind me of a sexist pig I used to know."

Blake turned on his heel without a word and walked out to the car. He didn't look back once as he climbed in and drove down the driveway and out of her life.

By the time Sienna and Georgie arrived to recap the day, Ana had wiped away her tears and washed her face. She tried to block out all the feelings that had resurfaced since last weekend. If she was honest, they'd always been there, and she'd buried them when she'd left Blake's house ten years ago. But this last week had proven that they were still opposites in every way that mattered, and a relationship just wouldn't work even if he did reciprocate her feelings.

She spent half an hour roaming around the house, packing up and putting away things that had been lying around for months.

Amazing what you could achieve in one day.

Garden weeded, living room and kitchen tidy, and the love of her life banished with a couple of unkind words.

Love of my life? Jeez, where did that come from?

By the time the girls came through the front door, a bottle of champagne in Sienna's hand, Ana was calm and composed. Sienna went straight to the cupboard and peered inside.

"Champagne glasses? I'm not drinking French champagne out of a vegemite glass, Ana."

"In the living room." She waved one hand in the direction of the old Welsh dresser.

A loud pop followed by the gushing of froth from the top of the bottle had Georgie running over with a glass. "Ugh, don't waste it. It's *Moet.*"

Ana frowned at Sienna. "A tad extravagant, considering we've only got one job lined up so far?"

"But we have news." Sienna grinned at her and Georgie clapped her hands. "Lots of news."

"Okay, spill. The news, not the wine." Ana grinned and tried to ignore the regret that was still tugging at her. She'd been perfectly happy before she'd met Blake again and she was going to be happy again.

Sienna poured the wine slowly, and Ana tapped her hands on the back of the chair impatiently. "Come on, girls, don't keep me in suspense."

Sienna handed her a glass and lifted hers for a toast. "Here's to the new *Sunshine Coast Reno Service*—" she paused and put out one hand in a dramatic flourish— "and to the feature of the Bennett's house in *Ocean Home* magazine."

Ana gasped. "Are you kidding me?"

Sienna nodded smugly.

"Oh, my God." Ana waved her hand in front of her face as a feeling of light headedness stole over her. "Either this champagne is potent, or I'm overwhelmed."

Sienna put her glass down and hugged her. "See, Ana. I told you it would all work out. Change is not all bad. The Bennetts want us to sign the contract for the restoration of a second house next week. And Georgie has news from the store, too."

"It was a good day, Ana. It's a shame you didn't stay for it." Georgie tipped her head to one side. "Blake's a honey. If he wasn't taken, I'd be going for him myself."

Ana's head flew up and she stared at Georgie. "Taken?"

Georgie laughed and nodded with a knowing glance at her sister. "Anyone can see you are head over heels, and we saw the way he looked at you in the bar the other day."

The heat started in the pit of Ana's stomach and travelled up her neck to her cheeks. She waved her hand in front of her face again as both girls laughed.

"It's the champagne." She glared at them. "Why was it such a good day?"

"Generous payouts for the staff who are going. Pay raises and great benefits for those who stay. Joe and Magda didn't stop smiling all day."

"That's good. I'm so happy for the staff—and you too, Georgie. Ana reached over and hugged her friend. "But our department was still destined to go. I'm just pleased the Bennetts made the offer before we got fired." She picked up the bottle and topped up her champagne. "Sounds like Blake was a hit."

"He was great. He talked about how he believes the store should keep its local identity and how he would work hard to keep that."

"I'll believe that when I see it."

"You're too hard on him, Ana. What did he ever do to you?" Georgie frowned at her. A ripple of guilt flickered through Ana. Georgie always saw the good in every situation. Or maybe Blake was coming around? Maybe he'd begun to understand what their community was like? And what it meant to her?

Ana wandered over to the window and spread her fingers on the cool glass. The rain had cleared, and the sun was hovering above the horizon as the day came to an end. Soft pink and gold hues filled the western sky and tinged the mountains with a soft light. She sipped at her champagne and the bubbles tickled her nose.

"You're right, you know. He's just doing his job." She turned back to the twins. "After we see the Bennetts on Monday, I'll go into the store to see him." Going over to the table, she tapped the lid off one of the shoeboxes. "Besides, I promised Joe I'd get these invoices to Blake by then."

Sienna looked at the boxes on the table and laughed. "I'll believe that when I see it."

"I have every intention of clearing the backlog before Monday." Ana put her champagne glass down. "That's my weekend plan."

Chapter Thirteen

Ana sat back in her chair and lifted her arms above her head, stretching her neck from side to side, trying to ignore the beautiful day outside. The mid-morning sun was streaming through the kitchen window heralding the onset of summer, the birds were screeching in the bush and Mutt sat at her feet, his big brown eyes telling her he would love a walk in the hills.

"One more box to go and we'll go for a walk," she promised. His tail thumped on the floor and she reached down to rub his head. "But there'll be a lot more time spent doing the books from now on, boy."

She'd not slept well. After the girls had gone home, she'd worried about the huge step she and Sienna had taken. From now on, they would be on their own, and excitement warred with common sense in Ana's thoughts. She had a horrible feeling their decision to start their own renovation company had been made in haste and if it hadn't been for Blake's comment about Joe making a killing on the Bennett job, they would have waited to see what ensued in the meeting with him at the store.

He just didn't understand.

Ana fought back the thought that maybe—just maybe—what they'd been doing for the past few years hadn't been good business. But when she looked at Thelma and Mitzi, and the other locals they'd helped out, they'd done a damn good job and made a lot of people happy.

They would never have been able to afford to do the work for the community without Joe's generosity, and their hard work. Could they fund it all on their own? Perhaps not right away, but eventually? She reached for the final box and lifted out a handful of papers. Mutt jumped to his feet and ran to the door and for a moment, she thought he'd given up waiting and was asking to go out.

And then she heard the purr of a motor. The same sound of the car that had been driven out of her driveway so abruptly yesterday.

Prickly heat ran up and down her body as she looked down at her pyjamas. Standing up quickly, the antique Hitchcock chair crashed to the floor behind her and she shut and locked the front door before scurrying back to pick the chair up.

Oh God, she'd already insulted him. Now he'd think she was slamming the door in his face. Ana opened the door again, peering around the side.

What on earth is he doing here?

Blake walked around the back of the car and opened the passenger door. Ana watched with fascination as he held his hand out and Maddy emerged from the back seat, the ever-present book tucked beneath her arm.

Ana turned and ran up the stairs to her bedroom pulling off her pyjama top along the way. By the time she was in her room and searching desperately for a clean T-shirt and a pair of jeans, a knock sounded at the front door.

"Be down in a minute," she called out.

Low voices drifted up to her as she quickly washed her face and pulled a brush through her hair. Finally, she slipped on a pair of flat shoes and walked slowly down the stairs, to catch her breath and compose herself.

When she stepped out onto the porch, Blake was sitting in one of the rocking chairs with Sooky who was once again on his lap. Maddy was crouched in front of him stroking the cat's long, silky fur.

"Well, hello, Maddy." Ana threw a guarded glance toward Blake. "This is a lovely surprise."

"Hello, Ana." Maddy stood and clasped her hands together in front of her chest. "Uncle Blake and I are going on a picnic. Will you come with us? Please?"

Before she could answer, the little girl rushed on. "We didn't have one when Billy was naughty in the park when Mummy was helping Daddy in the rainforest and Mummy said we could have another one today and Billy could stay home, and Benny and Roddy are at soccer and—"

Blake placed his hand on Maddy's shoulder and interrupted his niece. "And Uncle Blake thought it would be a really good way to show Ana how friends can have a good time together?" He lifted his sunglasses and met Ana's gaze. "Even after they argue?"

"Well . . ." Ana eyed Blake for a moment and a pleasant shiver ran down her back as he held her gaze steadily.

"We are still friends, aren't we?" he asked. His head was tipped to the side and he raised his eyebrows. More often than not he'd been the one to initiate the peace between them in the past, and it looked like he was trying to make amends now. The laugh lines around his eyes deepened as he smiled. He was still the Blake she'd held close in her heart and the ice around her heart cracked a little more. She looked away from him reluctantly, and down into Maddy's earnest little face. "I guess we are."

Maddy gave a whoop of delight and turned her attention back to the cat.

A tentative smile tipped the corners of Blake's mouth up. "Maddy was really excited to see you again. You made a big impression last weekend."

Blake glanced at his niece and then he walked along the porch to Ana. "I wanted to see you too, but I wasn't sure what sort of reception I would get." He kept his voice low and Ana inclined her head for him to follow her into the house.

She stepped inside and waited as he closed the screen door behind him.

"Blake—"

"Ana—"

They both spoke at the same time and Ana smiled.

"Me first," she said. Blake leaned on the door frame and waited for her to speak.

Blake smiled at her and she tried to ignore the trembling that shot down her legs. It was only because she'd run up and down the stairs in about twenty seconds.

That was all.

"I shouldn't have left the store without talking to you. That was rude." He'd made the first move and she was happy to give a little.

Blake held up his hands. "Let's call a truce for the day. There's a little girl out there who's had a bit of a tough week."

"Oh, no. What happened?"

Blake took a step back and looked out to check on Maddy. "It's been a big week for the whole family, with Rod's accident. And on top of everything, some kids at school gave Maddy a hard time. Jeannie thought a change of scenery would do her good." He held his hands out and said simply. "So here we both are. Two needy souls."

Ana burst out laughing at the plaintive look on Blake's face. "That's the last thing I'd call you, Blake. You're the most self-sufficient person I know."

Blake grinned back at her and then caught sight of the invoices spread out over the table. He raised a quizzical brow at Ana. "You know you don't have to do them anymore."

"I promised I would finish them. No regrets and no hard feelings."

Blake stepped closer to her and the fresh smell of soap filled her senses as she dropped her gaze. His denim jeans were faded but neatly pressed with a sharp crease running down each leg. He reached over and tipped a finger beneath her chin and tilted her head up gently.

For a moment, she thought he was going to kiss her again and she was disappointed when he spoke instead.

"We still need to talk about work, but not today, I promise. Today is for having some fun." The crinkles around Blake's eyes deepened as he smiled at her. "And catching up on that picnic Maddy missed out on."

"Sounds good to me, where are we going?"

"The Fairy Pools in the National Park. Lots of tidal pools there for Maddy."

Ana looked down at her clothes. The heat rose in her neck as she realised her T-shirt was on inside out and her jeans were crumpled from being on the bedroom floor all week.

"Just give me a minute?"

***

As they travelled down the highway, Maddy showed off her excellent reading skills. Blake glanced back affectionately as her little voice confidently read the words about the littlest lighthouse keeper. A soft marshmallow feeling lodged in his chest as he glanced across at Ana. She was quiet, and she looked out at the ocean as he steered the car along the coast road. When she'd come back downstairs, his breath had caught in his throat. She'd changed into some sort of loose, floaty dress and her silvery blonde hair was down around her shoulders. It was just as though they'd gone back ten years and the hippy college student had come back.

"I thought we'd go to the beach first and have our picnic before we go for a walk. Maddy would like to collect some shells too." He turned the car into the National Park car park. "Okay with you girls?"

"That's fine with me. I'm just tagging along as a guest." Ana smiled at him and stretched her head back to look at Maddy who had finished reading the story. "This is a great beach, Maddy. Have you been here before?"

The little girl shook her head. "We don't go to the beach very much because the boys can't swim, and Mummy says you need too many eyes." Maddy counted on her fingers. You would need six pairs of eyes to watch us." She was quiet for a moment as she kept counting on her fingers and then looked at Ana with wide eyes. "Wow, that is twelve eyes plus ours. That makes twenty two eyes all together. So that would be all of us kids and Mummy and Daddy and you and Uncle Blake and we would still need two more grownups to get enough eyes."

Blake glanced across at Ana and grinned. Her eyes were almost as wide as Maddy's.

"Do you know why you need so many eyes, Ana?" He laughed when she shook her head. "One pair for each child and a spare—just in case."

Ana opened the door and waited by the car as Blake helped Maddy out, before he opened the trunk and lifted out a huge picnic basket and a rug.

He passed the rug to Ana. "Maddy, you hold Ana's hand. I need both hands to carry this basket. I think Mummy thought that all the eyes would be coming when she packed our lunch."

As Ana turned to his niece and held out her hand, the light wind lifted her hair. The neckline of her dress was scooped and a tantalizing glimpse of the soft swell of her breast peeked out. Blake forced himself to look away and hefted the basket up.

"Come on, girls. Time to go exploring." His voice was gruff and when he glanced back, he caught Ana's eye. For a moment nothing more was said. Clear hazel eyes looked back at him, calmly assessing. Perhaps seeing more than he'd wanted her to see until they'd sorted out what was happening between them—without the complication of the store takeover making things difficult.

That damned patchouli she wore wafted around him when she moved, and it reminded him of that night they'd had together. If he closed his eyes, he could still feel her silken skin beneath his fingers. It had been such a long time ago.

Too long.

"Uncle Blake, why are your eyes shut?"

"Ah, I was just having a rest." He turned to Maddy. "Come on, there's lots of starfish, urchins, and hermit crabs for us to look for."

When he and Jeannie had been small, their parents had brought them here to the rockpools on many weekends and it was fun to be doing it again with Ana and Maddy. He had a wonderful memory of swimming to his dad unaided for the first time as a six-year-old in the big pool and calling triumphantly to this mother and Jeannie who watched from the rocks. That was what he wanted from life.

Those moments of love and sharing of happiness.

The restlessness of his corporate life didn't compare to moments like that. For years he'd kidded himself that Jeannie and Rod and their kids were enough family for him. But when Ana's clear assessing gaze locked with his, the certainty of the future he'd mapped out for himself faded.

Ever since he'd kissed her the other morning, his world had shifted, and he was going to do his damnedest to convince her he wasn't the greedy businessman she seemed to think he was.

Slow and steady.

All he had to do was convince her of that.

They walked down along the bush track to the beach before the pools, and Maddy shrieked with delight as the velvety sand squeaked between her toes. Blake found a sunny spot sheltered from the wind off the sea, tucked the picnic basket beneath an overhanging rock, and covered it with the rug. The morning sea mist had burned off, and the sun was warm on his back as he followed Maddy and Ana along to the Fairy Pools. Ana's dress blew against her slender figure and he watched her, wondering if there was a possibility of a future together. He stood back and looked north as Maddy led Ana from one tidal pool to another and the little girl's excited chatter didn't stop.

Blake dropped to a crouch and waited for them to come back to him with their bounty. He looked curiously at the crustaceans Maddy held in her cupped hands, before looking up at Ana. Her fair cheeks were flushed, and her expression, contented.

"Ready to eat?"

She nodded and walked back to their picnic spot while he took Maddy back to the water to carefully place all the creatures back in the pools. By the time they got back to the sheltered spot beneath the bluff, Ana had spread out the picnic rug and was peeking in the basket.

"Oh, yum. I forgot to have breakfast." She grinned up at him. "Too busy playing with shoeboxes."

Her sense of humour filled him with anticipation. Maybe she wasn't going to hold a grudge. Reaching into the basket, she passed him three picnic plates before lifting out some sealed containers.

"Potato salad, green salad, quiche and oh, I wonder who this is for? A peanut butter and jelly sandwich?"

Ana handed the sandwich to his niece and Blake grinned.

Maddy giggled. "No, that's for Uncle Blake."

Ana shook her head and passed over the sandwich with a laugh. "Had me fooled."

Blake leaned back against the rock and the warmth seeped through his T-shirt as he munched on his sandwich. "I've got more places for us to see, girls."

'Where to?' Maddy asked.

'Not far from here,' he said.

'You sound like you remember the area well.' Ana said.

"I do. What would you say to me becoming more of a local than just running the store?"

"How?"

He spoke slowly and kept his attention totally focused on her reaction. His future happiness—and hers if things went as he planned—depended on how she took his news.

"I plan on living here for more than twenty-five years. I'm keeping my house on the canal, but I'm moving to Maleny."

Chapter Fourteen

The gloss of the day rubbed off a little for Ana after Blake dropped his news during their picnic lunch. Up until then she'd managed to put all thoughts of work out of her mind. They were just two friends and a little girl having a fun day out together.

Blake put the picnic basket and rug back in the car after they finished lunch and they strolled along the track back to the car park and crossed to the other side of the next bluff. A large pod of dolphins frolicked in the waves and Maddy's delight made the long walk worthwhile. As the path became a little rough, Blake held his hand out to Ana. She tried to ignore the frisson of nerves that travelled up her arm at his touch.

As they watched the dolphins, Blake held Maddy up high and Ana held her phone up until the little girl stopped squealing.

"Smile, Maddy," she called, taking longer than necessary to capture the shot.

No man should be so good-looking. Standing in front of the brilliant blue water, he looked so strong and sexy. His plain white T-shirt hugged his broad chest and his faded jeans clung snugly to muscular thighs. By the time Maddy insisted on taking one of Blake and Ana, Ana was well and truly flustered, and she stood stiffly in the circle of Blake's arm, pasting a smile on her face. His hand rested low on her back and as they stood, waiting for Maddy to take the photograph, the light pressure of his fingers sent a delicious shiver down Ana's spine. As she trembled, Blake's fingers began a slow caress on her lower back and by the time Maddy yelled 'smile', he had moved his hand around her and pulled her close against him.

"Have to make sure we're both in the frame for Maddy's photo." His warm breath whispered close to her ear.

"Another one," Maddy yelled as she stepped closer to them.

After Maddy had taken the photo and walked back to them, Blake kept his arm loosely around Ana's shoulder and she had relaxed against him.

Maddy nodded off to sleep as they headed back to town.

"Do you want to go for a coffee after we drop Maddy home?" Blake asked quietly.

Ana glanced at her watch. "Drop me off first. I need to get home. I'd like to take Mutt for a walk before the sun goes down."

"Okay. I've got an appointment in town tonight."

An appointment or a date?

Ana wondered which it was, but Blake didn't say any more.

Rich. Good looking. A great house—make that *two* great houses. She was sure the women would be falling over his doorstep to hook up with him.

Maddy was still asleep in the back when they reached Hill Cottage and Ana quickly exited the car.

"Don't get out, Blake." She walked around to the driver's side and he slid his window down, reached out and took her hand. Ana looked down at his strong fingers wrapped around hers.

She squeezed his fingers lightly despite wanting to pull back as confusion filled her. "Thanks for a fun day."

"What are you doing tomorrow?" Blake lifted her hand and brushed it against his lips.

The question surprised her. "Why?"

"I'd like to drive back up and see you. There are a few things I still need to talk to you about."

"Oh. What sort of things?" Excitement rippled through her at the thought of him wanting to see her again so soon.

"I'd rather leave it till tomorrow when we can have a proper talk."

"I'll call you. I'm not quite sure what my plans are yet."

"Okay. I'll be down at the store anyway, so I'll look forward to your call." He dropped her hand and then turned to her again. "Watch that Mutt dog of yours, while I back out."

Ana bent down and picked up Sooky before whistling for Mutt.

"And Ana? Thanks for your company. Maddy was really excited you came along with us." After a final wave from him, the window slid up and he backed slowly down the drive.

Ana stood with her hands on her hips watching until he turned the car onto the highway, and they disappeared. She walked slowly inside.

It had been such a great day. Not one cross word spoken, and she'd enjoyed his teasing. She'd seen yet another side to Blake today and wondered if that was the real Blake that had been buried under the business exterior. When he'd dropped the bombshell the was moving to Maleny her thoughts had been in turmoil. He'd be close by, and living in such a small community, she'd be sure to run into him often.

It was going to be hard to remember he was the new boss at Home and Hardware.

##

As it turned out, the next day didn't go as planned. A frantic call from Joe's cousin, Maria, sent Ana hurrying into town to help with the shingling of their roof. Her elderly husband, Aldo, had started the job while Maria was at church and she had come home to a fallen ladder, a husband stuck up on the roof, and a great gaping hole above her kitchen.

Ana packed the ute, slipped on her dungarees, tool belt, and work boots and drove the short distance into Maleny.

Maria was waiting for her outside and folded her in a grandmotherly hug.

"Thank you, Ana. Look at the silly old fool. I told him to call and get you to do it."

With her hands on her hips, Ana called up to Aldo. "Having a bit of trouble up there?"

A frown and a grunt were all she got in return.

"Let the silly old man sit up on the roof for a while. Come in for some *biscotti* and lemonade." Maria bustled ahead of her toward the front porch, but Ana shook her head.

"No, I'll get up there and help before he hurts himself. It shouldn't take too long." Ana picked up the ladder and wedged it firmly against the edge of the garden before joining Aldo up on the roof. The morning fog had been heavy, so Ana took extra care as she slid over the slippery roof shingles toward the elderly man.

She grinned. Below them, the gaping hole opened to the kitchen and she could see Maria at the stove as the tempting aroma of minestrone came wafting up.

"Morning, young Ana." Aldo's voice was gruff.

"What seems to be the problem?" Ana looked across the tops of the houses toward the hardware store on Main Street. At least if she needed any gear to help Aldo she could go and get it.

No, she corrected herself. She would have to go and buy it. Her work was no longer a part of the store and that was going to take some getting used to.

"I've loosened all the old glue, but I can't lift the shingles around the edge of the hole." Ana looked down at Aldo's old gnarled, arthritic fingers, not surprised he couldn't get a firm grip on the material.

"No matter, I'm here now with my tools and we'll get it done in no time."

Aldo insisted on climbing up and down the ladder to get the replacement shingles two at a time and Ana bit her lip in worry each time he disappeared over the edge of the roof. It took four hours to glue the new material in place. Maria insisted they come down for lunch and that had added another hour to the day.

The final shingle was placed, and she wiped the last bit of excess glue with a rag. She turned to follow Aldo across the roof as Blake's car slowed to a stop and parked behind her.

Her heart gave a funny little flip when he stepped out and leaned against the bonnet of the Mercedes. She sat on the peak of the roof and waited as Aldo climbed down the ladder.

Blake grinned up at her. "Are you coming down or should I come up there?"

Here she was sitting on a roof in her old work clothes, and all it took was the sound of Blake's voice to make her heart beat faster. She seriously needed to get over this . . . and him.

"I'm coming down now," she said.

She could see the grin on his face, and she closed her eyes to block out the sight. He strolled leisurely across the pavement to the ladder and put his hand out to help Aldo down the last few rungs. Ana was acutely aware of her bottom at his eye level as she climbed down the ladder and ignored the jolt that ran up her arm as he took her hand to help her down. It was bad enough that her legs turned to jelly when he'd pulled up, now her arms were all tingly from where he'd touched her. She jumped down onto the concrete path, her work boots making a resounding thud as she landed.

"Aldo, this is Blake Buchanan. He's the new manager of Joe's store."

The two men shook hands before Aldo disappeared inside to wash the glue off his hands.

"Well . . ." Blake said.

Ana stared at him. He was dressed in his faded jeans teamed with a black T-shirt today, and it highlighted his dark hair. Sunglasses covered his eyes, and his lips were turned up slightly, but he didn't seem happy now.

"Well, what?" She stood with her hands on her hips. "Is something wrong/"

"Is this how you usually spend your weekends?"

"More often than not. Do you have a problem with that?"

"You work too hard." He finally lifted his sunglasses, and she returned his look with the same intent that was in his.

"I don't class it as work. I like to help my friends."

"So it's not a paying job?

"I don't think that's any of your business. I don't work for the store anymore, remember?"

"Truce?" Blake held his hands up in front of him. "Honestly. I was just interested."

Ana relaxed her stance and slid her hands from her hips as he went back to his car and opened a rear door. Turning away she unclipped her tool belt and slipped it off, before walking to the ute and shoving the belt through the open window onto the front seat. She took a deep breath and composed herself before turning back to him. She gasped in surprise and raised her fingers to her lips as Blake handed her a posy of violets wrapped in mauve tissue paper. She raised them to her face and inhaled the sweet fragrance.

"I saw these as I drove into town and I thought of you. A peace offering?"

Warmth surged through Ana and she kept her eyes down, for fear he'd see the hunger in her gaze. "Thank you, that was very thoughtful." She placed them carefully on the front seat. "I just have to say goodbye to Maria and Aldo and then we can have our chat."

"Can I follow you back to your place?"

"Okay."

Ana's stomach grumbled as Maria pressed a pot of soup and a cob of freshly baked bread into her hands. "Thank you so much."

The old, wrinkled face beamed at her. "You are a good girl."

Ana hugged Maria. The women in the community had banded together when her mother had passed away and had looked after her. It was like having a huge family of elderly aunts—and uncles— and she was always glad to help them out. She glanced up to see Blake watching them with a kind smile. Hope filled her and she held her breath.

He is beginning to understand. Please.

She followed Blake's car along the road until they both turned up her driveway. Anticipation and doubt about talking to him warred for supremacy in her mind.

After today, she probably wouldn't see much of him.

And it wouldn't bother her one bit.
Really.

He would be immersed in running the store, and once she and Sienna signed the contract with the Bennetts, they would be busy with the next house.

Blake was waiting for her on the driveway as she pulled up and he walked over and opened her car door.

"Thank you."

He didn't speak. Mutt ran over to greet them both and Sooky nudged Blake's leg as they walked along the porch together and he gave her a quick pat.

"Come in." Ana unlocked the door and gestured for Blake to follow her inside. He stepped in past her and she pushed the door shut. Before she could speak, Blake moved in close and put his hands on the door behind either side of her head. Her heartbeat quickened with anticipation as he held her gaze.

He lowered his head slowly and his mouth touched hers lightly. She hadn't known her body could feel so alive until his soft and coaxing lips claimed hers and she clung to his shoulders and kissed him right back. His T-shirt was bunched in her fists and heat spread from her fingertips. It coursed through her, and the slow, steady flame grew until she felt she would burn from the heat filling her entire body.

All her thinking, and worrying, and doubt disappeared for a moment as their lips met and clung.

And then the doubts crept back in and reason damped the heat.

Reason which was cold and empty.

Ana stiffened and pulled back and Blake loosened his grip. Running her hands through her hair, she looked up at him, surprised to see his cheeks flushed and his eyes hazy. She was sure she looked the same.

"I've wanted to kiss you again since last weekend," he said softly. "It's all I can think about."

"Why?"

Ana swallowed and lifted her head to meet his intent gaze. He grinned at her and she clasped her hands to her chest.

"Because I can't get you out of my mind." He shook his head. "I'm supposed to be concentrating on this move—horrendous as it is—all I can think about is you."

"Horrendous? Which move? The store or the house you bought?" Ana dropped her arms as the warmth dissipated as quickly as it had filled her.

"You didn't have to do either, you know. Things could have stayed the way they were."

Blake crossed the room and stood at the large window overlooking the ocean. "Change can be good, Ana."

She followed him over and stood next to the antique rocking chair which she had positioned to take in the view.

"How? Why can it be good?" She knew she sounded like a petulant child, but her emotions were in turmoil and she didn't want him to know how her blood was still zinging from his kiss.

"Life moves on. People change. Our needs change." The earnest expression on his face was the same as when they'd argued in college. But this time, she was listening to him . . . just a little bit.

"You have to be honest and really think about what it is you want out of life. Too often we get caught on the work treadmill. I know I did. The move here—reconnecting with my family—has been the best thing for me. When my parents died, I thought making my fortune would fill the gap I felt. But I was wrong." He shrugged and held his hands out to her. "It didn't. The move home and meeting up with you again—that's shown me what's important. . .and what I want. What I need."

He stretched his hands out to her and she stared at them for a moment before wiping her palms on the front of her dungarees. Her own hands were dirty, and her nails were broken from pulling the shingles off the roof. Slowly, she reached out with one of hers, as tentative acceptance of his words. He raised it to his lips, and she couldn't help the smile tugging at her mouth.

"Let's take it slow. Let's start afresh and get to know each other again. No baggage, no past?" Blake tipped his head to the side and he quirked an eyebrow. "We've had the truce, now we'll make a deal."

"Before we start talking mergers?" She chuckled at the look on his face. "Always the businessman, Blake?"

"All depends on what sort of . . . er . . . mergers you are talking about. I can think of a few pleasurable ones myself."

Her face heated as Blake slid his hands along her arms and pulled her close. She snuggled into his warmth and sighed with pleasure as he leaned his forehead against hers. His warm breath puffed on her cheeks for a moment before he slid his lips slowly down her cheek until they teased at the corner of her mouth. Ana shivered, her lips parted, and she waited for his mouth to claim hers again. The thought of a 'merger' sent spirals of heat shooting through her limbs.

Her eyes flew open as his phone rang stridently. Blake pulled back reluctantly and lightly touched her face.

"I'm sorry. I'm expecting a call that's going to make a big difference to things." He brushed his lips across hers. "Hold that mood?"

Ana stepped back and pointed upstairs before he took the call. "That's fine. I'll have a shower and get changed. Would you like to stay for some of that minestrone and bread Maria sent home?" He smiled and nodded before turning away to speak into the phone.

Ana went out to the car to bring in the food and put the gas on low beneath the soup pot. She glanced across at Blake as she headed for the shower, but he was frowning and intent on his conversation.

Standing beneath the hot jets, Ana could barely contain her excitement as she scrubbed at her hands to remove the dirt and dried glue. She quickly rinsed her hair, before exiting the shower and drying herself off. She wrapped the towel around her as she searched for something to wear.

Muttering to herself, she discarded the underwear at the top of the basket in her closet and dug deep for a pink lacy push-up bra and matching panties. A soft pink cashmere sweater and a draping skirt completed the outfit. A quick spray of her patchouli perfume and a dash of lip gloss, and she was ready to go back down. Her stomach fluttered and she looked in the mirror again. Her eyes were bright, and her lips were softly parted.

Yes, this is right, and you will give it your best shot.

A merger. Hmmm.

Walking slowly down the stairs, her legs trembled with anticipation and she listened for Blake's voice, but all was quiet— it seemed his call was finished. She hurried into the kitchen and turned the soup down and placed the loaf of bread in the oven to warm.

"Almost ready," she called.

He didn't answer. Ana walked into the living room, but the room was empty. Smiling to herself, she opened the front door and called out to the porch. "Are you hungry?"

All was quiet. Mutt lifted his head and flopped his tail on the tiled porch and Sooky ran over and wrapped herself around Ana's legs, meowing for her dinner.

The space beside her ute where Blake had parked was empty. Disappointment filled her chest as she walked back inside. A note was propped up against the shoe boxes on the table.

'Sorry something came up. Will call.'

And that was why they would never be any good together, she thought sadly. Business had always come first with Blake—and it always would. He couldn't even wait for her to come downstairs to tell her he had to leave.

Chapter Fifteen

Three days passed and there was no call or visit from Blake. Ana tried to tell herself she didn't have time to think about it, that she didn't care.

On Monday, she and Sienna met with the Bennetts and came to an agreement for two more restoration jobs. On Tuesday, they spent the day at the houses, measuring and making lists. Today, she and Sienna were back at her cottage, planning out their work and ordering the supplies they would need.

Ana moved to the table which was now clear of shoeboxes and picked up their new order book. She'd dropped the boxes at Georgie's house on Sunday night and asked her to take them into the store for her on Monday. It was the worry of the new business venture that was keeping her awake at nights and waiting for the phone to ring through the day.

And constantly checking that her phone was not turned off.

Nothing to do with Blake.

She was waiting for jobs to come in. That was all.

"We can only order exactly what we need," Sienna commented. They were at Ana's cottage and stood at the window looking out over the hills. "We don't have the luxury of everything at our fingertips anymore."

Ana nodded absently. She glanced down at the phone and resisted picking it up to check for messages.

"You okay, Ana?"

"Yes, why?"

"I thought you'd be happier." Sienna looked at her expectantly.

"Why?"

"Oh, just that Maria was telling Georgie about the hunky guy who came to see you when you were fixing Aldo's roof." Sienna tipped her head to the side. "And he gave you flowers?"

Ana looked at the posy of violets on the kitchen windowsill. They were starting to wilt. "Oh that? Blake just stopped by to say thanks. For helping him out."

She'd been all excited about telling Georgie and Sienna how things were panning out with Blake until he'd disappeared. Now she wasn't game to put what she felt into words in case she'd read him all wrong.

"Yes. And?"

"And nothing."

"Why should there be an 'and?'"

"Because I know you very well and there's something bugging you. Is it because Blake's gone away?"

Ana's head flew up. "Gone away?

"Yes, he went to Melbourne first thing on Sunday night. The takeover's been put off for another week. Didn't he tell you?"

"He doesn't have to tell me anything, Sienna. I don't work there and I'm nothing to him."

Obviously.

"Ah. . . so that's the way the wind blows." Sienna smiled. "Georgie will be upset if you beat her to a wedding."

"Oh for goodness' sake, Sienna. Stop talking nonsense." Ana pushed some catalogues across the table to her friend who was looking at her too intently. "Sit down and start looking for some ideas for the Bennett's beach house. If we are going to make this business a success, we have to make this project spectacular."

Sienna looked at her from under her lashes. "And if we are going to make this business a success, you have to do away with shoebox accounting."

Ana swatted one of the catalogues in her direction and laughed when Sienna ducked.

***

Blake stood outside Mike's executive suite in the building near Federation Square and cursed himself for the umpteenth time. He couldn't believe he'd left his mobile in his car at home before he'd caught the taxi to the airport. He'd tried everything he could think of how to find Ana's number but none of his attempts had come to fruition. He couldn't call Joe's store and ask for her number because negotiations were at such a delicate stage. He didn't know Georgie and Sienna's last name so he couldn't look them up. And Ana's number still wasn't listed, just like it hadn't been ten years ago. Damn it all.

He pushed open the door of Mike's suite. The secretary gestured to a chair. He felt bad about leaving Ana's place while she was in the shower. The note he'd left for her had been brief but when the call came in from Mike, he'd only had an hour to get to the airport. His whole attention had to be on the meeting ahead—any chance of a future with Ana hinged on the next few minutes. If things went as planned, he would have plenty of time to make up for the way he'd left her.

She'd be fine.

She'd forgive him.

He hoped.

"Come on in, Buchanan." Mike's voice boomed through the door and his secretary jumped. "Are you waiting for an invitation?"

Mike sat behind his huge cherrywood desk and glowered at Blake as he entered the office. Being called by his surname did not bode well. Mike steepled his fingers in front of his chin and stared at him.

"Sit down."

Blake nodded at the man who had been his boss for the past three years. "Thanks for seeing me at such short notice."

"I'm disappointed in you, Blake."

"I appreciate you considering my proposal, Mike."

"I think you're crazy, you know. You had a bright future with this company." Mike shook his head. "In fact, I'd even hoped you might buy me out when I was ready to retire. That son of mine doesn't want it."

"You never know, he might change his mind," Blake responded kindly, though in truth he knew Jack was happy with his sculpture.

Mike reached over and stabbed at the buzzer on his desk. When there was no response he yelled through the open door. "Grace, bring those papers in here." Then he stood up and called out loudly. "Please."

"Of course, sir." The secretary walked in and placed a file on Mike's desk. "Will there be anything else, Mr. Devereaux?

Blake smothered a smile. It wasn't just him who found Mike difficult. Grace went back out to her desk.

"Coffee, Blake?"

"No thanks, Mike. I've got a plane to catch."

"Don't know what's gotten into you, boy." His soon-to-be former boss shook his head and hollered through the door again. "Grace. Get Jim to come up, will you. We need a lawyer to witness this."

##

Ten minutes later, the papers were signed and as Blake walked to the door, Mike stood and threw his arm around his shoulder.

"Anytime you want to come back here, there'll be a job waiting for you."

"I'm pretty settled out on the Sunshine Coast now, but thanks for the vote of confidence." Blake punched Mike playfully on his burly shoulder. "And anytime you want to come and visit, I've got that great big house on the canal at Noosa. Lots of guest rooms.'

He didn't want to mention the move to Maleny in case it jinxed things.

Mike turned to him, his face sombre. "Seriously, Blake I hope it all works out for you. You never were one to take things slow. And I guess Helen will want to go up and visit Jack, so I might take you up on that offer one day."

Blake stepped out on the street and whistled for a taxi. As he headed to the airport for his return flight, he felt lighter than he had in years.

Ten years to be precise. And it felt so good, it was worth the wait. And his life was about to get even better.

Chapter Sixteen

According to Georgie's grapevine, Blake was still away, and Joe was stomping around the store like a cranky old man. Ana spent the whole week running from one place to another in the whirlwind of the new business and her house descended back into its normal mess. Sienna and Georgie had dragged her into Caloundra to purchase a laptop that was now set up in the small room off her kitchen. A ceremonial burning of the shoe boxes, which Georgie returned *sans* accounts, took place out in the garden on Thursday night with a bottle of wine to toast the signing of the Bennett contract.

This morning was spent at Thelma and Mitzi's house where Ana finally finished painting their kitchen. Sienna painted a *trompe l'oeil* of a cow in a field on the bottom half of their kitchen door and they all stood back to admire it.

Ana giggled, and whispered behind her hand to Sienna as the elderly ladies stepped closer and pored over it. "It's awful."

"Ssh," Sienna hissed. "It's what they wanted."

"It's the eyelashes." Ana kept a straight face as Sienna elbowed her and they were both smiling a few minutes later as they walked to the ute.

"Give me a lift home? I walked down," Sienna said.

Thelma and Mitzi stood at the door and waved to them as Ana backed down their driveway.

"Say hello to your young man for us, Ana." Mitzi called out.

"Bring him over to see us soon," Thelma added.

Ana put on a dramatic eye roll for Sienna's benefit and tooted the horn at the old dears. "I love this town, but it has a crazy rumour mill. There is nothing between Blake and me."

"Oh, come on, Ana. You are so transparent. You've been mooning around all week like a lovesick cow, and as soon as someone mentions Blake's name you are at instant attention. That's what gave me the idea for the cow's eyelashes." Sienna laughed. "I love it. I'm trying my hand at sculpture too, life's been a bit boring lately."

Ana didn't reply and turned down Main Street toward Sienna's house. She was desperate to know when Blake would be back but didn't want to give Sienna more reason to tease her. Finally she couldn't hold back any longer.

"I wonder when Blake will be back from Melbourne. Do you know what it's all about?" She kept her attention on the road in front of them, trying to inject a casual interest into her voice.

"Georgie said something's going on at the store but it's all a big mystery. The takeover was supposed to be signed off by now, but everyone has just been told to come to work as normal until Blake gets back, even those who got their notice." She looked at Ana with a sly grin. "And no, I don't know when that will be."

"Okay. You're right, I'll admit it. I am attracted to him. I always have been but it's not going anywhere because we are too different."

"Opposites attract, you know." Sienna crossed her arms and sighed. "Don't let him go because of a foolish belief."

"It's not foolish. Blake has always put business first. I never have. So I have to get over him and move on."

"Just because your views lean toward the charitable side, don't judge him too harshly.

Ana thought over Sienna's words after she dropped her off at her house. Before she headed out to the cottage, she decided to stop by the store and see Joe. It was strange not to be there every day to pick up gear. It had been her second home for ten years and the staff were like her family.

She parked the ute in the back and hoped Blake's grey Mercedes might be there, too, but there was no sign of it. After she saw Joe and Magda, she was going home for a long walk in the hills with Mutt. Sienna's words had stuck in her mind and she knew she had a lot of thinking to do.

Maybe Blake had taken off in a tearing hurry the other day because he'd regretted kissing her.

Maybe he'd given their relationship a lot of thought, too, and recognised how different they were.

Maybe he'd looked around her cottage when she was upstairs and realised they were poles apart. Her mess would frighten anyone away.

Slamming the ute door shut, she pulled herself up short.

Forget the maybes. From now on, she would take things as they came and when she went for a walk this afternoon, she'd figure out just what she was going to do and how she'd greet Blake when he came back home.

If he even came to see her.

But he had kissed her, and her insides went to jelly as she remembered that kiss. She grinned to herself. Sienna was right. It was just like being back in high school.

Ana slipped in the back door of the shop and greeted Herb, the security man, who was dozing in a chair by the back counter. If she was honest, there were a few places where the store could be improved.

Maybe it *was* time for change.

Georgie was manning the cash register and raised her eyebrows at Ana.

"Blake's not back yet."

Ana let out a soft groan.

"How many times do I have to tell everyone, there is nothing between Blake and me?" She pointed up the stairs to Joe's office. "Are Joe and Magda upstairs?"

"Yes, they're just back from lunch at Renzo's."

Ana was three steps up when Georgie called out to her.

"Ana?"

She paused and looked back to a broad grin on Georgie's face. "Yeah?"

"Don't pick pink for my bridesmaid's dress. It clashes with my red hair."

Ana stomped up the stairs and ignored the laughter coming from the counter below. Magda was sitting at the small front desk and she bustled around and embraced Ana in a close hug.

"Ana, my dear. We have missed you." She called into the office through the open door. "Joe, we have a visitor."

Ana stepped back and shrugged. "It's only been a week."

"But it's not the same without you and Sienna popping in all the time to pick up things and helping out. Is it, Joe?" She turned to her husband who had come to the doorway. He held his hand out to Ana and she followed him into the office,

"It is good to see you. Come in and tell me all your news." He winked at her and tapped his nose. "I believe you have some."

"Oh, not you too, Joe." Ana's face burned with embarrassment.

He tipped his head to the side quizzically with a gentle smile. "I heard something about the Bennetts. Is there something else?"

"Oh. No. That's all. Sienna and I have signed the contract so it's public knowledge."

"Ah, that is good." He nodded. "There have been a lot of enquiries about your work since the Bennett place was sold."

"That's right."

"Blake was very impressed with your work, I hear."

"So he is still taking over the store?"

Joe sighed and ran his hand over his bald head. "Yes, the store takeover is going ahead." He smiled at her. "But it's all good news and I can tell you, there will be a lot of happy people in our town—including you, Ana."

Before she could ask the questions forming in her mind, the telephone on Joe's desk rang. When he ignored it, Magda called out from the small office.

"Joe, pick up. It's Blake and it sounds important."

Joe's eyes widened and he reached for the telephone. "Blake. Has it fallen through? Ah, I see. Yes. I can do better than that." He looked across at Ana and his brow creased. "Just a moment."

Joe turned to Ana with his hand over the hand piece.

"He wants your phone number." The old man frowned. "It sounds urgent."

Ana caught her breath and held her hand out for the phone. "I'll talk to him."

"Blake?"

"Oh, Ana. Thank God, I found you." Ana's legs trembled as Blake's voice broke. "I need you. Can you come to Noosa?"

She gripped the phone to her ear and her hand shook.

"What is it, Blake?" Her voice cracked as a dozen scenarios flicked through her mind. "What's wrong?"

"Billy's missing."

Chapter Seventeen

Before they disconnected, Blake gave Ana Jeannie's address. His flight from Melbourne had just landed and there had been a message for him. He'd made a frantic call to Rod; Billy had been missing for two hours.

As the taxi headed for Jeannie's house, all Blake could think of was the fear that had gripped him when Billy had run to the edge of the road at the park. He knew Billy's fascination with water. He stared out the window and clenched his jaw, trying not to think of all the lagoons near Jeannie and Rod's house. "I like to swim, *Unca* Blake." His throat clogged with emotion as he remembered Billy's determination.

Blake closed his eyes. As soon as the initial shock of Rod's call had subsided, a deep need to have Ana with him had filled him. He'd done a lot of thinking on the flight and he'd already decided to go and see her as soon as he got home to tell her his news.

Now that was all unimportant and he just wanted her by his side as they searched for Billy. Nothing mattered except Billy being found safe—and soon.

The taxi pulled to a halt outside Jeannie and Rod's house. Rod was home with the children and Jeannie was out searching with the neighbours. Two police cars blocked the driveway, and a news van was parked on the sidewalk. Neighbours stood in small groups talking quietly. The driver parked behind the news van and Blake grabbed his bag from the trunk before sprinting for the front door.

Rod must have been watching because the door opened before Blake was up the steps. His face was white, and he inclined his head to the living room.

"The kids are watching TV with one of the neighbours." Rod used his crutches to limp through the living room to the kitchen and Blake followed. Two women were in the kitchen making sandwiches and Rod smiled briefly.

"Bronwyn, Vivienne. This is my brother-in-law, Blake."

Blake nodded at the two women as Rod shut the door to the living room. "I don't want the kids listening. Maddy is really distressed. She blames herself because she was on the deck reading when he went through the side gate from the back garden."

"Tell me what's happening. Where should we look?" Blake pulled out a chair for Rod and took the crutches from him as he sat down.

"I feel so useless with this leg." Rod rubbed the back of his neck, his anxiety obvious in every movement. "Jeannie and two of the neighbours headed off to the paths along each side of the canal while I called the police. There's been no sign of him yet."

"The other kids are all here?" Blake hadn't even taken notice of who was in the living room as they walked through.

"Yes, but there is one good thing." Rod gripped the side of the table and his knuckles were white. "Jaws is missing, too. So we're just praying he's with Billy."

"Which gate did he get through?"

"One of the side gates was open. The one closest to the canal."

Blake swallowed. "You've searched the house?"

"Yes, and the yard and the neighbours' yards. Now we're waiting for the police with the search dogs to arrive."

"Where do you want me? Here with the kids or out looking?"

Rod dropped his head in his hands. "How about you drive me around? My keys are on the hook next to the garage door. You get the SUV out and I'll meet you out front."

Blake passed him the crutches and headed for the garage. He opened the garage door with the remote control on the wall and slid into the driver's seat. Backing the car out slowly, he parked it in the driveway. Rod was standing next to a policeman who was talking into a radio and for a brief moment, Blake hoped there might be news. He turned the car off and stepped out onto the driveway and waited for Rod to finish talking, his stomach churning.

A familiar sound of a rattly diesel reached his ears and he looked up as Ana's ute rumbled down the wide street. She parked it and ran across the lawn to him. Blake held out his arms and she ran into them.

He buried his head in her hair and the familiar patchouli fragrance filled him with comfort.

"Oh Blake, have they found him yet?"

Blake shook his head, unable to speak for a moment. "No, not yet." He cleared his throat and kept his arm tightly around Ana as Rod limped over to them on his crutches.

"Rod, this is my. . . friend. . . Ana. She's here to help."

Rod reached over, briefly shook Ana's hand, and then looked at Blake. "Are you ready?"

Ana stepped out of Blake's embrace "Where's Maddy and the boys? Would you like me to stay with them?"

Rod nodded and pointed inside without speaking before he handed Blake his crutches and stepped up into the car.

"Thank you for coming." Blake looked down at Ana and despite his worry, her presence calmed him. She stood in front of him chewing on her lip, her work dungarees covered with paint and more splotches of bright green paint on her hands.

"I'm so happy you called me."

"I need you, Ana. But we'll talk about that later." He dropped his head and kissed her hard, before throwing the crutches in the back of the car and jumping in beside Rod.

***

Ana walked past the colourful shrubs in the front garden and hurried up the stairs. She pushed open the front door and followed the sounds of the television. A middle-aged woman was sitting on the sofa cuddling a sleeping Jake. Ana walked over and lightly touched the baby's head.

"Hello, I'm Ana. I'm a friend of the family," she said quietly.

"Hi, I'm Sophie. I'm from next door."

"How are the children doing?" Ana whispered.

"Maddy's really the only one who knows what's going on. She wanted to go with Jeannie, but Rod asked her to stay here and help me with the boys. Now that you're here, I'll take Jake upstairs to his cot."

Ana slipped onto the sofa next to Maddy. "Hey sweetie."

Maddy looked up at Ana. Her eyes were wide, and her little chin was shaking. "Hello, Ana. I lost Billy."

The little girl's guilt broke her heart. "Oh no, you didn't Maddy. It's not your fault."

"I shouldn't have been reading my sea creatures book."

Ana held her arms open and Maddy slid over the sofa and nestled into her chest. The twins lay on the floor still engrossed in the cartoons on the television.

"You smell funny."

"I've been painting. My friend and I painted a cow on a door. I'll take you to see it one day. How would you like that?"

Maddy nodded. "How about today? As soon as Billy comes home?"

The backs of Ana's eyes ached with the tears she was holding back. "Well, we'll have to see what Mummy says."

Maddy nodded. "Can we go and play outside? Billy might have come back?"

Ana looked down at the twins. "As long as we all go outside together. It's my job to look after you while Mummy and Daddy and Uncle Blake are out. . . finding Billy."

"It won't take long," Maddy said. "He's got Jaws and he's got his iPad. They'll be able to hear them and then they can bring him home."

Ana squeezed the little girl closer to her. "That's really good thinking, Maddy."

"Can we look outside, too?"

"We sure can." Anything to keep Maddy occupied would help the little girl stop worrying about her little brother.

Please God let them find him before dark.

Ana switched the television off with the remote control and was met with a duo of disappointed cries.

"Come on, boys, we're going outside to have an adventure."

"How about a picnic?" Benny asked.

"Sure, let's see what we can find in the kitchen."

"All right, I s'pose that's okay." Roddy reluctantly pushed himself to his feet. "Can we have Coke at our picnic?"

"We'll see. You'll have to show me the way out to the back garden."

"It's not the garden. It's the jungle." Roddy's little voice piped up. "I'm going to be an explorer. Benny, you have to be the lion."

Ana averted the brewing disagreement as Benny opened his mouth to protest.

"Come and show me the jungle," she said.

The children led Ana through to the kitchen and she met a couple of neighbours who were making sandwiches for the search teams. Sophie had come down from the baby's room and was pouring coffee into mugs on a tray.

"We'll bring your picnic out." One of the women called as the children ran ahead to the door. Then she dropped her voice to a whisper. "No news?"

Ana shook her head as she turned toward the door. The back of the house was just above ground level with a huge wooden deck from one side to the other. The twins jumped down the two low steps and disappeared into the garden where thick bushes and high shrubs screened the high back fence. Soon their excited cries reached Ana and Maddy.

"Do you think it would be all right if I sit in the hammock and read?" Maddy looked up at Ana with her big brown eyes wide and her face serious. Ana's eyes pricked with tears and she pulled her sunglasses from the top of her head to cover them before Maddy could see she was upset.

"That would be fine."

Ana crossed to the edge of the deck and listened for the boys as they darted in and out of the bushes. She kept an eye on Maddy who quickly became absorbed in her book. Behind the fence she could hear the drone of traffic on the nearby bridge. A faint but familiar sound hummed beneath the traffic and then stopped. Ana cocked her head to listen but all she could hear was the traffic and the twins yelling in the garden.

"Maddy?"

"Yes?" The little girl gazed across at her.

"Did you say Billy had his iPad?" she asked softly.

"Yes. Why?" Maddy's voice was wary.

"Come on over here and sit down here with me? Tell me what you can hear?" Maddy slipped out of the hammock, her book dropping unheeded to the floor as she came over to Ana who had dropped to her knees. She lay down and placed her ear against the wood deck. Maddy kneeled beside her and together they listened. After a moment, the faint sounds of *Baby Shark* music drifted up.

And then it stopped.

"Maddy, is there a way to get underneath here?" Ana asked urgently. She bit down on the excitement filling her chest, not wanting to get Maddy's hopes up.

"There used to be a door, but Daddy locked it. Jaws took his bones under there and they smelled bad."

"Can you show me where?"

Maddy led her down the steps and around to the side of the house. A small shed filled the gap between the side of the house and the fence but Maddy pointed around to the back of the shed.

"It's behind there."

Ana squeezed through the narrow gap and bent down until she could see the small door. She pushed it, and it opened with a squeak. Turning to Maddy who was close behind her, she grasped the little girl's shoulders and held her gaze.

"Maddy, I have a very important job for you. Run inside and get Sophie and ask her to come straight out and watch Benny and Roddy until I come out."

Maddy looked at her and nodded.

"Can you do that for me now? Run fast." Maddy ran and Ana dropped to the ground and pushed through the small space. It was so narrow she had to turn her shoulders to squeeze through, but she was soon rewarded by the sound of a deep, low woof. As her eyes adjusted to the dark, a faint light flickered ahead of her in the far corner. A loud swish and a rush of air preceded the licking of her face by a rough tongue.

***

Blake and Rod had driven around every street within a two mile radius. Just before the bridge, they came across Jeannie, striding ahead of a group of volunteer searchers.

"Pull over, please," Rod asked. "Make her come home with us. She'll be exhausted. There are plenty of teams out there now."

Blake stopped the car and jumped out. "Jeannie."

His sister ran across to him and Blake's heart clenched. Her face was streaked with tears and he wiped a smudge of dirt from her forehead.

"Have they found him?" Her voice broke and he held his arms out to her.

"You need to come home with us. Rod's in the car. There are plenty of search teams out. You should be home so you're there when they find him and bring him back." He kept his voice upbeat, but Jeannie looked up at him and shook her head.

"He's in the water somewhere, Blake. He would have headed straight for the water."

Her legs gave way and Blake caught her and helped her across to the car before opening the back door for her.

Blake clenched his jaw and tried to block out Jeannie's sobs as he drove them back to the house. The feeling pressing on his chest was a hundred times worse than when he had watched Billy teetering over the traffic on the edge of Peninsula Park. He pulled into the driveway and retrieved

Rod's crutches from the back seat before going across to check in with the police coordinator on the front lawn. The policeman simply shook his head and Blake turned to the house, following his sister and her husband.

The living room was empty, and Jeannie called to the children.

"They're probably out back. Don't panic." Rod said.

She clutched the kitchen bench and doubled over. "Oh, God, where is he. . .?"

Rod limped to her and his crutch clattered onto the floor as he held her close.

Blake walked to the sliding door that opened to the back deck, surprised to see the three women gathered on the back deck and peering around the corner. There was no sign of Ana or the children.

"Rod." He frowned and kept his voice quiet. "I'm just going out to see Ana and check on the kids."

The twins were on the swing set and there was no sign of Maddy or Ana.

He walked up behind one of the women he'd been introduced to before. He didn't remember her name and he smiled apologetically. "Where's Ana?"

"She's under the house." The woman's voice was full of excitement. "Bronwyn's just run around the front to get the police."

"Rod, Jeannie, come quickly." Blake called through the door before he jumped down the two steps and went around the side of the house. Maddy was peering into a small gap behind the shed and as he watched, Ana wiggled out bottom-first and lay on the ground with her arms stretched out through the small gap.

Joy filled him, and he blinked away the wetness in his eyes as her soft voice reached him. "If you pass it out to me, I'll go and plug it in, and you can play *Octonauts* inside."

Billy's head poked through the gap and he handed the iPad to Ana. He crawled out closely followed by Jaws.

He looked up at Blake and called out.

"Hello, *Unca* Blake. Can we go to the park while my iPad's charging?"

Behind him, Jeannie shrieked and pushed past Blake, grabbing Billy in her arms, and folding to the ground. Blake swallowed as she cried and buried her face in Billy's hair. Rod limped over and stood behind them reaching down to touch his little boy's head.

Ana slowly pushed herself to her feet and walked toward Blake. Jeannie grasped her hand as she walked past and looked up at her, her face full of gratitude and her eyes awash with tears. Blake held her unwavering gaze as she walked slowly over to him. Her paint-splattered dungarees were filthy where she'd lain in the dirt beneath the deck and there was a wet streak of dog slobber on her cheek.

He'd never seen anyone more beautiful in his whole life.

He held out his arms and Ana stepped into them. Holding her close, her body curved into his and he captured her lips, not caring who was watching. He had never wanted anything more in his life than he wanted Ana at that moment. Her soft lips opened beneath his and she took what he offered. Something passed between then, something so elemental he couldn't put into words. Deeply moved, he cupped his hands around her damp cheeks and deepened the kiss.

Slowly she pulled back, and looked up at him, smiling. When she gazed up at him like that, a lump filled his throat as happiness surged through him.

He knew they would be okay.

***

Ana looked at Blake and took a deep breath. Two hours had passed since she had found Billy. The police had packed up and gone, the TV news team had their feel good story, and the neighbours had all drifted back to their respective homes. Jeannie was sitting on the sofa, still holding Billy close. To his dismay, his mummy had followed him around and had not left his side since he'd crawled out from beneath the house. He glared up at her.

Blake had stayed close to Ana, even following her into the bathroom while she'd scrubbed the dog drool off her face. "I guess I should think about heading home," she said softly.

"I was hoping you might drive me back to my place so I could pick up my car and some clean clothes. I'm going back up to the hotel at Maleny and my car's at home."

"Do you want to come with me to keep me company? I could drive you back down to Noosa at the end of the week." Ana looked down, embarrassed as Jeannie nudged Rod and smiled. This was all too new for her to take in. She looked down at her hands and picked at the bright green paint that was still stuck to her fingers.

"I guess I could do that."

Maddy came running over. "Can I come too and see the cow now?"

Ana reached out and hugged the little girl.

"How about tomorrow?" She looked across at Rod and Jeannie. "How about you all come? It's Saturday and we could have that picnic we keep missing out on?"

It was agreed, and Blake and Ana headed outside after making their goodbyes. Blake glanced across at Ana with a grin as she crunched through the gears.

"I need to talk to you," he said. "I have some big news for you."

"Not while I'm driving. Can it wait till we get back to my cottage?"

Blake reached over and rested his hand on her knee. "I can wait for however long it takes."

Chapter Eighteen

Ana waited in her ute while Blake grabbed some things from his house. He'd asked her to come inside but she preferred to stay in the car, scared they'd get side-tracked if she went with him. When they finally got around to having this talk, she wanted to be at her cottage. Being on her own ground would add to her confidence.

"Are you sure you don't want to take my car?" Blake threw a small bag onto the ute tray.

"No, I'll need the ute over the weekend. I promised—" she let her voice trail off— she knew how Blake felt about her doing odd jobs for the old folk.

"Keep going," he said. "You promised?"

"Doesn't matter."

He shrugged and held up his mobile. "Were you upset when I didn't call?"

"No," she lied through her teeth. "I thought you must be busy."

"Ana, we need to be totally honest with each other. Otherwise we have no chance."

"Blake, I don't want to talk in the car. I need to concentrate on driving." She reached over and turned the radio on.

"Well, just so you know. I left my mobile in my car before I went to Melbourne and I didn't have your number. That's why I didn't call."

She smothered a smile as relief shot through her.

The silence was comfortable as she headed up the mountain road, the rush of the wind through the open window and the loud music blaring from the radio covering up the usual roar of the old diesel ute as it laboured up the hills. Every so often, Blake would look across at her and smile. Anticipation curled in her stomach.

"Do you want to come back to my place before I drive you to the hotel?" Ana leaned over and turned the music off as they approached Maleny.

Blake reached over and took her hand with a smile.

"I'd love to."

Mutt greeted them as the ute trundled slowly up the driveway and sniffed her legs curiously as she stepped from the car. Ana reached down to fondle his ears.

"It's okay, boy. You're still my number one dog."

Her heart was pounding as Blake followed her along the porch. She opened the door and turned, drinking in the sight of him as he smiled down at her.

"If I go up and have a shower will you promise you'll be here when I come down?" She looked at him from beneath lowered lashes as shyness filled her.

"I promise." A smile lit up his whole face and she ran upstairs to the shower before her legs could turn to jelly.

The same pink lacy bra, the matching panties, the pink cashmere sweater, and the soft floaty skirt completed her outfit. Her hand shook as she pulled her damp hair back into a ponytail and applied a dash of lip gloss. She walked slowly down the stairs.

Blake stood by the window waiting for her. "All set?"

She nodded and sat primly in the chair beside the window, her back straight and her knees together. He crouched down and kneeled in front of her.

"Ana, I've got two things to tell you and then I want to ask you something."

Ana's heart was pounding, and her lips were dry. She resisted the urge to lick them and focused on his face instead as he looked up at her.

He reached for her hand and she was surprised to feel his hand trembling slightly.

"I have some big news and I think you'll be very happy."

It was like looking through a rosy haze and Ana giggled. "I think you could tell me anything now and it wouldn't upset me."

"First, I went to Melbourne this week."

"I know."

"I met with Mike and he agreed not to take over the store."

Dismay filled her. "Oh, no. Joe will be so disappointed—and Magda won't be able to go on her cruise."

Blake held her close and his lips pressed against her forehead. "That's one of the things I love most about you, you know. You are such a giving person. You always think of everyone else before yourself."

Ana shook her head. "So what's happening? Are you out of a job? Oh no, you've bought the house here. Where will you work? Where will you live? What are—?"

"Sssh." Blake put his fingers on her lips again. "Listen to me."

Ana frowned and considered all the implications of the non-takeover. "But—"

"I bought the store."

"You what?" For a moment she thought Blake said he'd bought the store.

"I bought the store. Joe and I are signing the papers on Monday."

"You bought the store?"

Blake beamed down at her. "Yes."

"You bought the store?" Ana's breath hitched as she repeated the question.

"You've already asked me that. I'm looking for someone to do a renovation job for me. Someone who can bring it into the twenty-first century but keep that old hardware store atmosphere. Do you know anyone who might be able to do that?"

"Oh my God." Ana gazed up at Blake as she struggled to keep her voice steady. She was so happy she couldn't understand why tears were pricking at her eyes. "How does Sunshine Coast Renos Service fit into the scheme of things? Will a local firm fit the bill?"

"I think they'll fit in very well," he said, and his smile got wider. "I think in a community like ours. . ." Blake paused, and joy shot through Ana as he made himself a part of her community. "In a community like ours we have to stay local."

She grabbed his hands and brought them up to her face unable to put her joy into words. Blake raised her fingers to his lips as he held her eyes with a true and steady gaze.

"Ana, I let you go ten years ago without realising how I felt. I've searched for happiness since then, but I was always unsettled. As soon as we met again, my life felt complete." He held her gaze. "The second thing I want to tell you is the most important. What I want to tell you. . . is how much I love you."

She drew in a quick breath and opened her mouth to speak but Blake placed his fingers gently over her lips.

"Let me finish. What I want to ask you is. . ."

Ana closed her eyes, as the joy and love for this man surged through her. For the first time, she was able to accept her feelings and knew they were returned in full.

"Open your eyes."

Slowly she met his gaze and smiled as her heart settled into a slow steady beat, as steady as the love shining from his face.

"Will you marry me, please, Ana?"

Nothing could overcome the love she had for this man.

She met his gaze full on. "If you'd asked me the same question ten years ago, I would have said no. If you'd asked me a week ago, I would have been slow to answer. But..."

She leaned forward to let her lips touch his, her heart aching with love, with need, wanting to feel him against her. Against his mouth, she murmured the words in her heart. "But now. . . no hesitation, no second thoughts . . . yes, Blake. I'll marry you."

He leaned in and kissed her, and a thrill coursed through her as his arms pulled her close. She'd waited a long time for this moment, but it had been worth the wait.

Epilogue

Mutt and Jaws hit it off as soon as Rod opened the back of the SUV in Blake and Ana's garden and the bloodhound had jumped out, ears swinging in the breeze. It was a warm October afternoon and the sun shone from a brilliant blue sky with not a sign of cloud on the mountains. The whisper of the wind stole ruffled gently through the trees and Maddy and Rod were down on the lawn throwing sticks to the dogs.

Sienna lounged in a garden chair while Georgie bustled around offering drinks to the guests sitting at the tables scattered through the orchard. Thelma and Mitzi had made lemonade for the ceremony.

"Roddy! Benny! Get down at once." Jeannie called out to the twins as they climbed high in one of the orange trees. She hurried over and stood beneath the tree, one hand grasping Billy's shoulder, the other holding on to Jake who was toddling along beside her.

One final car came up the driveway and Joe and Magda, and Maria and Aldo walked through the gate. Georgie ushered them through to the orchard.

Georgie called out to Rod and Maddy and they walked up the cliff path. Rod's hand was on his daughter's shoulder and Maddy had a huge grin on her face.

Maddy ran into the house along the porch.

"Everyone's here now," she called happily. "You can come out."

The door opened and Blake stepped out first, closely followed by Ana who was holding the newest resident of Maleny close to her chest.

They walked slowly to the orchard and Blake looked down at his wife of eleven months with a huge grin rivalling that of the bloodhound who was lolling on the end of the porch. A laugh rippled through the small crowd as the celebrant met them at the gate and held her hands out for the baby dressed in little dungarees with a pink ribbon in her hair.

"Welcome, Faith Anastasia Buchanan."

THE END

Did you like Ana's story?
Sienna and Georgie's story are available too.
Sienna's story in The Trouble with Jack,
and
Georgie's story in Healing his Heart.

Sienna's story starts on the next page.

Sienna's story

The Trouble with Jack

Chapter One

The door of the Sea View Gallery at Noosa Heads shut with a satisfying *click* behind the last customer of the day, and Sienna Sacchi turned the closed sign around on the glass door.

"I thought she'd never leave." She yawned as she looked over to the electrician who was waiting to show her the new lighting he'd installed in the front corner of the gallery.

"But she was loaded with bags with the gallery insignia on them, if I'm not mistaken?" Jeremy waited for her to come over to the counter. "You were wasted in restoration, Sienna. You're a born saleswoman."

Sienna had been friends with Jeremy since school; the other business Sienna was involved with hired him for the electrical work. The restoration business—or house flipping as Georgie preferred to call it—was shared with Georgie, her twin sister, and their best friend, Ana, up the mountain at Maleny. As well as working with the girls until recently, Sienna had also worked part-time in a small gallery up the mountain until she'd seen the ad for the gallery down here at Noosa.

"And a talented artist, too, don't forget." Sienna grinned at him as satisfaction coursed through her. A sale like the one she'd just made reassured her that her decision to be a silent partner in the reno business and move on to focus on her art and buy this gallery had been the right one. She would be her own boss once again; working for someone else stifled her creativity. "And yes, she loved my enamelled frogs, and bought one for each of her friends back in Sydney."

The sale had been one of the biggest Sienna had made since she'd taken over the management of the gallery a month ago. Her hiring had been done by email with the company and she hadn't even met the owner—the soon-to-be former owner; the gallery administration operated under a company name. Once she owned the place, she would have final say in how it was run. She couldn't wait to tell the girls; she'd told Georgie she had news but wouldn't give any clues away.

"That's the sort of customer you want." Jeremy looked at her with a grin. "Holy Dooley, I saw the price tag on your frogs when I was running the electrical wires under the shelves."

Sienna nodded with a smile. "So, are you done?"

"I am. Are you ready to be bedazzled?"

"I am." Sienna had filled the corner at the front of the gallery with her own work. She waited as Jeremy stepped behind the elegant glass table she used as a counter, reached down, and flicked a switch.

Sienna gasped and put her hands to her lips as she surveyed the once-dark corner. The various little creatures came to life on the display shelves along the side wall. Colourful frogs peeked from behind small pieces of wood softly lit by downlights hidden beneath the higher shelves, and copper grasshoppers gleamed in the corners. She had been working day and night to finish her sculpted metal creatures for her upcoming exhibition, but she still had a lot of work ahead.

"Happy with the job then, sweets?"

"Happy? I'm delighted. It's like fairyland." The small creatures she had enamelled in bright primary colours were highlighted by the carefully placed lighting. She stepped closer and twirled around, looking at the lights as they twinkled, and was hard pressed not to yell out in delight. "You've worked magic, Jeremy. Thank you so much."

"My pleasure." He picked up his toolbox and crossed to the door. "I won't bill the company until I finish the whole room for your exhibition. Let me know when you want me to come back."

After he left, Sienna wandered around, barely able to keep the smile off her face. The gallery looked very different from when she'd taken over as manager, with an option to purchase, only four weeks ago. The last email from a secretary at the company advised that any changes she made before the contract was signed must be approved and then would be billed out to the company. It had taken three weeks to get the approval to go ahead with the lighting, and she'd worried it wouldn't be complete before her exhibition. As soon as she'd received an email giving her the go-ahead, she'd called Jeremy to come in to do the work, and he'd turned up within an hour.

There'd been no reply from her solicitor about the contract of sale when she'd checked her email at lunchtime; she glanced down at her watch. Hopefully it would settle next week, and then the gallery would be all hers with the freedom to do as she wanted before her first exhibition. Having to get permission to make any change, no matter how small, was a pain in the proverbial.

There was no time to check her email before she left for the restaurant. As usual Sienna was running late, and she knew the girls would tease her about being late for her own birthday dinner.

She grabbed her iPad and her bag from beneath the counter, and with one last satisfied smile at the beautifully lit display, she flicked the lights off and headed for the back door.

If you enjoyed Ana's story, you can find:
Sienna's story in *The Trouble with Jack,*
and
Georgie's story in *Healing his Heart.*

All available in Annie's bookstore in print
https://annieseatonstore.ecwid.com/

and on Amazon print store.

OTHER BOOKS from ANNIE

Daughters of the Darling
From Across the Sea
Over the River (2024)

Porter Sisters Series
Kakadu Sunset
Daintree
Diamond Sky
Hidden Valley
Larapinta
Kakadu Dawn

Pentecost Island Series
Pippa
Eliza
Nell
Tamsin
Evie
Cherry
Odessa
Sienna
Tess
Isla

The Augathella Girls Series
Outback Roads
Outback Sky
Outback Escape
Outback Wind

Outback Dawn
Outback Moonlight
Outback Dust
Outback Hope

An Augathella Surprise
An Augathella Baby
An Augathella Spring
An Augathella Christmas
An Augathella Wedding

Sunshine Coast Series
Waiting for Ana
The Trouble with Jack
Healing His Heart
Sunshine Coast Boxed Set

The Richards Brothers Series
The Trouble with Paradise
Marry in Haste
Outback Sunrise
Richards Brothers Boxed Set

Bondi Beach Love Series
Beach House
Beach Music
Beach Walk
Beach Dreams
The House on the Hill

Second Chance Bay Series
Her Outback Playboy

Her Outback Protector
Her Outback Haven
Her Outback Paradise
The McDougalls of Second Chance Bay Boxed Set

Love Across Time Series
Come Back to Me
Follow Me
Finding Home
The Threads that Bind
Love Across Time 1-4 Boxed Set

Bindarra Creek
Worth the Wait
Full Circle
Secrets of River Cottage
A Clever Christmas
A Place to Belong

Others
Whitsunday Dawn
Undara
Osprey Reef
East of Alice
Four Seasons Short and Sweet
Follow the Sun
Ten Days in Paradise
Deadly Secrets
Adventures in Time
Silver Valley Witch
The Emerald Necklace

A Clever Christmas
Christmas with the Boss

About the Author

Annie lives in Australia, on the beautiful north coast of New South Wales. She sits in her writing chair and looks out over the tranquil Pacific Ocean.

She writes contemporary romance and loves telling stories that always have a happily ever after. She lives with her very own hero of many years and they share their home with Barney, the ragdoll puss, who hides when the four grandchildren come to visit.

Stay up to date with her latest releases at her website: http://www.annieseaton.net

Awards

2023: Winner of the long contemporary RUBY award for Larapinta

Finalist for the NZ KORU Award 2018 and 2020.

Winner ...Best Established Author of the Year 2017 AUSROM

Longlisted for the Sisters in Crime Davitt Awards 2016, 2017, 2018, 2019

Finalist in Book of the Year, Long Romance, RWA Ruby Awards 2016 Kakadu Sunset

Winner ...Best Established Author of the Year 2015 AUSROM

Winner ...Author of the Year 2014 AUSROM

Best Established Author, Ausrom Readers' Choice 2017 Book of the Year